The
BILLOW
MAIDEN

JAMES DIXON

Illustrations by Tamsin Rosewell

THE BILLOW MAIDEN
is a GUPPY BOOK

First published in the UK in 2022 by
Guppy Books,
Bracken Hill,
Cotswold Road,
Oxford OX2 9JG

978 1 913101 725

1 3 5 7 9 10 8 6 4 2

Papers used by Guppy Books are from well-managed
forests and other responsible sources.

GUPPY PUBLISHING LTD Reg. No. 11565833

A CIP catalogue record for this book is
available from the British Library.

Typeset by Falcon Oast Graphic Art Ltd
Printed and bound in Great Britain by CPI Books Ltd

To Mum and Dad,
who told the first stories.

One

Things began to get bad over the last few weeks before the summer holidays. It was Ailsa's first year in secondary school, she hadn't long turned twelve, and her mum got ill. She began to spend every day in bed. The place became untidy, then outright dirty, and finally there was no food left in the fridge or freezer.

In the end, Ailsa had to phone Uncle Nod.

'It's happening again,' she told him.

'You hold tight, love,' he said. 'Pack your bags. I'll be there soon.'

He was there a few hours later. His truck chugged to a stop outside their flat. Ailsa ran outside to meet him, relieved. They half-carried Ailsa's mum out to the truck, lay her across the rear seats, and packed their bags into the back.

Uncle Nod looked over at Ailsa as they left the city. They took the motorway up to the harbour.

'Your aunt's getting your room ready for you,' he said. 'And Moxie knows something's up, daft old fool. He'll be dead excited to see you.'

'How long will we stay with you?' she asked.

'As long as you want to, love,' he said. He grinned over at her, though she could see how worried he was. She was worried too, but she felt safer now she was with him.

Uncle Nod drove them onto the ferry. He sat in the truck and her mum lay swaddled in a blanket across the back seats. Ailsa spent the whole time at the front of the boat, enjoying the sea spray and the wind. It was her favourite part of the journey. The choppy sea and savage wind, the bump and rock of the boat, and the salty, briny smell of the sea always made her smile. It always made her feel alive.

The island on which her aunt and uncle lived emerged on the horizon as she stood watching. It gleamed in the summer sunshine, and she relaxed a little bit.

Uncle Nod and Aunt Bertha would take care of things. They always did.

*

A couple of days passed, then a couple more, and Mum stayed shut up in her bedroom. Ailsa spent every hour she could out and about, exploring the island's coast. Uncle Nod gave her a torch and she had packed her wellies in with her other things, despite the summer's warmth. It was everything she needed.

That and Moxie, of course. She always felt better with Moxie around. Everyone did.

There were lots of different paths leading down to the island's caves. Each one led to any number of thin stretches of rugged beach. The beaches were all rocks and heather and washed-up seaweed. The caves were carved through the high cliffs that overlooked the beaches.

'This whole stretch of coast is riddled with them,' Aunt Bertha always told Ailsa with a smile. 'Smugglers and worse used them for centuries as hidey holes and what-not. But you be careful down there. Places like that can be treacherous for a landlubber like yourself.'

Water pounded the beaches every day as the tide rose and the wind whipped up. It was only ever safe to try them at low tide, so Uncle Nod also gave Ailsa a chart with all the tidal times written down. She read the chart

3

every morning in bed as she worked out when to take Moxie out exploring.

About a week into her stay, Ailsa walked Moxie along a particularly rocky cove. She doubted many people came down here. It was overgrown and poorly trodden. She had only spotted the path by accident, and even then, it was only because Moxie had run over to it.

Moxie ran off again, halfway along the cove. His tail wagged and he worked his nose hard, sniffing at a thin cave mouth in the rocks. It was almost hidden from view by great ropes of seaweed that clung to its edges. A slab of moss-slick rock led up from the beach. Waves washed over it, even during the low tide. Moxie ran up to it, giving a few short, sharp barks as he did so. Then he disappeared inside.

Ailsa didn't want to follow. The cave's smell was over-powering. It smelled like the fishermen who came to Uncle Nod and Aunt Bertha's yard in their overalls and wax coats, covered in fish guts and worse. It smelled like the harbour on a hot day when they brought their catches in. But Moxie wouldn't come back when she called him.

Ailsa carefully walked up the stony slab and peeped inside. Jagged rocks stood up everywhere. Everything

4

was dark and clammy, despite the day's warmth.

It was horrible, and there was more to it than the smell and the darkness. Ailsa felt a deep-rooted sense of sadness in her belly as she peered in after Moxie. There was no explaining it. Ailsa couldn't have done so had she wanted to. But it was there, dragging at her, making her feel miserable just looking. It was too familiar, just like their house became whenever Mum got sick.

She shone her torch in. Moxie whined from somewhere inside and she found him with the light's beam. She heard something moving, something faintly splashing.

'Moxie . . . ?' she ventured, but she couldn't see him.

'Ailsa!' a deep voice called out. She jumped back from the cave.

It was Uncle Nod, away along the coast.

'What are you doing, love?' he asked as she scrambled up the cliff path and jogged over to him. He pointed at the sea. The tide was eating its way up the beach. 'Tide's turned, lass!' he said. 'You'll get yourself drowned staying down there!'

'Aye, Uncle Nod,' Ailsa replied. She had been sure she was meant to have another hour or so before the tide turned. She whistled and Moxie came bounding out of

5

the cave and ran up the track to join them. Bits of seaweed stuck to his fur, and he was dripping wet. Great gobs of salty muck clung to his muzzle.

'Did I not tell you to keep an eye on the tide times, love?' Uncle Nod grumbled as they walked back from the clifftops.

Moxie hopped nimbly along beside them, looking very pleased with himself.

'Well?' Uncle Nod asked, stopping and turning to face her. 'Didn't I?'

Ailsa faltered. She stood before him, sun-kissed and wind-blown, dirty from the day. 'Aye, Uncle Nod,' she began, 'but I thought—'

'Well, heed me, child,' he snapped. 'We've enough to be getting on with, your aunt and me, worrying about your mum. You think we want you washing out to sea and all? It'd finish us all off, love.'

'Aye, Uncle Nod.'

'And you be careful on those rocks,' he said. 'Those cliffs are crumbling, falling into the sea. More go every day.'

'Aye, Uncle Nod.'

'Well, then. Good,' he said. 'You keep a closer eye on these things. On the tides themselves. They can be fickle when they want to be. Your grandad used to tell me often enough. Fool as he was, he knew the way of things. Keep an eye on the time and tide, and the rest will take care of itself, he'd say. You could do with thinking on that.'

'Aye, Uncle Nod.'

He glared at Moxie. 'And you, boy,' he said. 'You should know better too, dragging her off down there.'

Moxie hung his head.

'Aye, then,' Uncle Nod said. Then he smiled. His face split into craggy joy. 'Come on with you,' he said. He turned and beckoned for them to follow him home. 'I've got dinner to start, and an extra pair of hands never went amiss.'

'Aye, Uncle Nod.'

Ailsa and Moxie followed along. A sharp wind buffeted the coast and the caves as they left.

Two

Ailsa stood in the kitchen peeling and chopping onions, carrots and potatoes. Uncle Nod was busy seeing to the fish. He filleted and seasoned it and clattered about, making a lot of noise. Aunt Bertha came in. Her overalls were splattered with dark grease and white paint from the yard. There was a smear of oil across one of her cheeks. She and Uncle Nod always had oil everywhere, under their fingernails, over their clothes, in the creases of their knuckles.

'All set?' Aunt Bertha asked.

'Aye, love, nearly there,' Uncle Nod replied. He grabbed the plate of vegetables from Ailsa and slid it all into a pan of boiling water with a stock cube and a sprinkle of salt and pepper. Then he diced the fish up and put it in and started slicing and buttering bread.

Ailsa only ever had fish like this when she came to stay with her aunt and uncle. At home, fish was fried in bread-crumbs or batter. It came with chips and Coke from the place on the corner. Here, it was fresh out the sea each morning, a point about which Uncle Nod was always very proud.

'And if it's that fresh and that good, you treat it right,' he once told her. So, he had a big book of recipes for different kinds of fish meals. He liked to show off when people came round, Aunt Bertha always said.

Aunt Bertha washed her hands as clean as they would get and sat down heavily at the table. 'How's herself, then?' she asked, jutting her chin at the ceiling.

'Sleeping,' Uncle Nod replied.

Aunt Bertha nodded and looked at Ailsa. 'You seen your mum today?' she asked.

Ailsa shook her head and came to sit next to Aunt Bertha.

Aunt Bertha placed a hand on her shoulder. She smelled of grease and boats and new sweat. 'Sorry it's all so much,' she told Ailsa. 'I know it's hard. You understand, don't you, hen?'

Ailsa shrugged. 'Aye,' she said. Sometimes she thought she understood. Sometimes she didn't. Right now, she didn't.

Moxie whined from the corner.

'That's enough from you, you daft wee beggar,' Aunt Bertha told him.

He slunk away to his bed.

The three of them ate dinner. Ailsa picked at her stew and drank a glass of milk. Aunt Bertha and Uncle Nod chattered away, but she didn't listen. She thought about home, about her mum. She thought about the sea and the beaches. She thought about the cave and the sense of sadness she had felt standing before it.

Her thoughts were interrupted by a knock at the door.

'I didn't realise how late it had got,' Uncle Nod said. He stood and hurried to the door. He came back a moment later with Dr Arbuthnot.

Ailsa didn't think she liked Dr Arbuthnot. He was too clean and too polished. He had a horrible, nasal voice that always made it sound like he was wheedling you. But there were no other doctors nearby who could treat her mum.

'And how are we all today?' he asked as he followed Uncle Nod into the kitchen.

Ailsa shrugged and drank the last of her milk and excused herself. 'I'll head out for a bit more while it's still light,' she told Aunt Bertha.

'Aye, then, hen,' Aunt Bertha said.

Dr Arbuthnot frowned but said nothing.

Ailsa left through the kitchen door, out into the back garden, with Moxie trotting along after her. He had become her shadow since Uncle Nod had brought her and her mum here. The garden overlooked Aunt Bertha and Uncle Nod's yard. Three upturned boats lay in a row. There were a couple of outboard motors opposite them as well as boxes and tools scattered about. The garden also overlooked a couple of other small houses and one big house, a little way up the lane. The village was visible just along the coast when the weather was fair, like today. The island's main town was hidden behind a large range of hills.

Ailsa and Moxie passed by the big house. She looked up at it. It was very grand and well kept. High walls surrounded it and electric gates shuttered it off from the world.

'That's the Galach place,' Uncle Nod had told her once, on a previous visit. Lots of the sailors and fishermen moaned about Mr Galach, the man who lived there with his family. Lots more were scared of him. He ran a couple of trawlers. 'Massive things that drag nets along the bottom of the sea, scooping up absolutely everything. Devils, they are,' Uncle Nod had said. 'Nobody else can catch a thing anymore. The Galach crews have taken too much. They keep taking too much. Now everyone else has to sail out for miles and miles to stand a chance of making a catch. Though that's not the worst of it. They're into all sorts of dodgy businesses, the Galachs. They're crooks, gangsters, the lot of them.'

'Aye?' Ailsa had asked.

'Oh, aye, they'll do anyone in for a profit,' Uncle Nod said. 'Violent criminals, the lot of them.'

As she walked past the Galach house, Ailsa heard somebody laughing on the other side of the high walls. She hurried past. She hadn't wanted to see much of anybody since she had come to her aunt and uncle's. Not this time. She was happier alone with her thoughts, alone with Moxie. Other people's fuss was too much right now.

Moxie hurried with her, trotting along at her side.

The tide was in, but the sun would last a few more hours yet. Summer sunset wasn't until late this far to the north. With Moxie's help, Ailsa found the slim trail to the cave and they both climbed back down. The surf covered everything except for the slab of rock heading into the cave's mouth.

Why am I here? she asked herself.

She was scared. She was shaking with it. There was no good reason at all to come back to the cave. But something about it repelled her and drew her in at the same time.

Ailsa could see the seaweed shimmering around the cave's slim entrance. Foam from the crashing tide flecked the front of the rockface. She tiptoed across the rock. Moxie fell into the water a couple of times, but he climbed out and shook himself down. He soaked her the second time. She half fell in at one point. One of her feet went in and she had to stop to empty out her wellie.

The smell of dead things and rotten fish washed over her as she got to the cave's mouth. It made her gag. The sadness welled up all around her, tugging at her heart and her stomach.

What on earth could it be?

Moxie raced in and she took a deep breath and followed, holding her nose, lighting her torch as she did so.

Stalactites thrust down from the ceiling, dripping and cold. Shadows and dark corners loomed at her. Her torch's light barely seemed able to cut through it. When she did manage to see something, it was generally some kind of dead sea creature decomposing where it lay, or else just hard rock. Moss and seaweed clung to everything.

It was too much. Her heart began to race, her palms began to sweat, and her knees went weak. She turned to go back every couple of steps, but each time Moxie nudged her forwards. Then he ran off a few metres into the darkness at the back of the cave. She gasped and ran after him, shining the torch's thin light forwards.

That's when she first saw the strange woman.

Ailsa screamed.

The strange woman was lying half in a rock pool at the cave's far end, with her legs and lower torso submerged. Her head was down, limp against her bare chest. She was covered in slimy, wet greenery and a few dead shells. Ailsa

14

passed her torchlight over her and saw that her skin was grey and pallid. Open sores puckered along her arms, chest and shoulders. Straggly, matted hair fell in tight ropes over her chest.

It looked to Ailsa as though the sea had spat her up and forgotten about her. She thought she was dead at first.

Moxie whined, however, and the strange woman stirred. She cursed. Ailsa gasped and leaped backwards.

'And who . . . on earth . . . are you meant to be?' the strange woman asked.

A grizzled mouth worked her words with an effort as though she hadn't spoken in a long time. Her voice was lightly accented and coarse. It sounded thin. She looked up. Her eyes blinked slowly, and Ailsa thought her teeth looked sharp, though she couldn't be sure in the darkness.

The sadness she had felt before rolled over her, deep and intense. It pulled at her. It was coming from this woman, she realised. Ailsa shivered and she couldn't speak, her heart hammering in her chest.

'Well?' the strange woman snapped.

Ailsa turned and ran, her nerve finally giving out. Moxie bolted along behind her. They crashed half in the water, half along the slab of rock, clambered up the steep pathway, and sprinted all the way home.

Three

Ailsa slept fitfully that night. When she did sleep, she had horrible dreams. The strange woman was there, in her rock pool. Then the sea rose up and covered the whole coastline. Seaweed and foam advanced onto the land. Water filled every cave and crashed down in a rising tide over the town and over Uncle Nod and Aunt Bertha's house. The whole island sank before the end.

Her mum was in one of the caves in her dream. She took off her clothes and lay down in a rock pool, half submerging herself. Then the cave filled with seawater, and she began to slip below the surface as Ailsa watched, drowning . . .

Ailsa woke up drenched. At first, she thought the sea truly had flooded the house and soaked her. Then she realised it was cold sweat. Her breath was fast and shallow and, for a second, she thought she saw the strange woman looming out of the shadows in the corner of her bedroom.

Moxie came trotting in, pushing through the door with his muzzle. He came over to the bed and licked Ailsa's fingers. His tail wagged and he whined gently in the back of his throat.

'Aye, good boy,' she breathed. Her throat was tight.

The wind howled outside and the whole house creaked. The first light was breaking for the morning. Far off, Ailsa could hear the first few fishermen banging about and calling to one another, getting themselves and their boats ready. Uncle Nod's snores rattled from his and Aunt Bertha's room, but they would both be up and about soon enough.

Ailsa got up. The alarm clock jangled as she and Moxie padded out into the hallway and Uncle Nod's snores turned into muffled grunts and curses.

Ailsa went into her mum's room. Moxie waited outside. He hung his head and his tail drooped.

Her mum was grey. Her eyes were closed and

completely still, their lids not even fluttering. She lay under a blanket, swaddled and almost entirely still. Ailsa thought she looked as though she had been frozen in time. The bed was across from the window and the morning's pale light shone through between a gap in the curtains. It shone like a halo around mother and daughter, though Ailsa thought it didn't bring any warmth.

Ailsa put her hand under her mum's sheets. She put her palm flat on her mum's chest and felt her heart beating ever so faintly. Her mum seemed small, like she had shrunk around her own bones. Ailsa knew she hadn't eaten properly in weeks, if not longer. She got like this every couple of years. She always had. No matter how old she got, Ailsa always found it terrifying. It never got any easier, though it seemed worse this time.

I found a strange woman in a cave and I don't know what to do . . .

Ailsa tried to speak. She tried to say something, to tell her mum all about it, to share the burden. She wanted some advice, to know what to do, how to help. She wanted to know how to deal with the fear and the sadness.

No words came. Her tongue felt thick.

Her mum stirred. She murmured and rolled over, away from Ailsa.

'Come on, love,' Aunt Bertha said from the doorway. She was in her night clothes. A sad smile crossed her lips as she watched Ailsa.

'Aye, Aunt Bertha,' Ailsa said.

'Let's leave her in peace, now,' Aunt Bertha whispered kindly. 'Come on, hen, I'll get us all some breakfast going.'

'Aye,' Ailsa said. She turned from her mum and went downstairs with Aunt Bertha and Moxie. She looked out of the kitchen window, out to the cliffs, as she munched her cereal. She imagined the strange woman down there, lying half submerged in the rock pool.

The docks were hot and busy. Ailsa took some sandwiches and a can of fizz down with her. She didn't want to be in the house, and she didn't want to go back down to the caves. Not yet.

There was a lot of fuss at the docks, of course, but folks were generally too busy to disturb her. She could get some peace and watch the world go by. She could think if she needed to.

Sailors marched back and forth. Their overalls were salt stained and grimy. She watched boats come in as she sat on the harbour wall, eating her lunch. She threw pieces of crust for Moxie to catch. The sun shone brightly, sparkling on the sea, catching the crest of each rising wave. Everywhere smelled of fish.

'You here to help, love?' one of the fishermen asked as he passed her by. He was wheeling a barrow, but his catch was small. Only a few fish lay in it, flopped on their sides with their eyes popping.

'I said, you here to help, love?' the man repeated. He grinned at her, goofy looking.

Ailsa shook her head. Then she went back to throwing crusts for Moxie.

'Aye, I was only joking, love,' the man said.

'Aye.'

'Not much to carry, anyways,' another fisherman said. He was passing by with a half-empty barrow. His eyes looked in slightly different directions to one another.

'Aye, well, it feels like the sea's plotting against us,' the goofy looking man said. He had kind eyes and shaggy whiskers and he winked at Ailsa.

'More like the Galachs are plotting against us, pal,' the man with the odd eyes said.

The goofy fishermen turned red.

'Quiet, you fool!' he hissed.

'Just saying.'

'Aye, well don't.'

The two fishermen carried on, wheeling their meagre barrows away past Ailsa and Moxie. They seemed to keep arguing as they went, though they did so in hushed voices. Ailsa watched them go, curious. She finished her sandwiches and threw a final crust for Moxie. She finished her drink and threw the can into a nearby litter bin. A ferry chugged along on the horizon, drawing closer, coming from the mainland. She watched as it cut through the water.

'Come on, boy,' she said, turning from the sea and the fishermen.

Moxie trotted along after her as she set off for Uncle Nod and Aunt Bertha's yard.

She walked up to the house, thinking of the fishermen's argument. It reminded her a little of school. There was a bully at school named Charlie. Nobody told on him, no matter what he did. He was too mean and too good in a fight. He tried to bully her once. She had sent him packing, but she was one of the only ones who could.

Boat parts and clutter lay all around the yard. There was some junk on either side of the gate and more as she went inside. Aunt Bertha was nowhere to be seen, but Uncle Nod was there. He was bent over the side of a small rowing boat. His tools were laid out beside him, and his face was red and sweaty in the summer's warmth. He looked around as Ailsa and Moxie walked up to him.

'Hullo, love,' he said.

'Hi.'

Uncle Nod gestured at the boat. 'One of those wee pleasure boats,' he told her, 'from the loch. Sprung a leak and it's tourist season and all.'

'Aye.'

'You seen your mum today?' he asked.

'Aye, this morning.'

'Aye, good. She needs us all, love,' he said.

'Aye.'

Ailsa waited for a few seconds, then opened her mouth.

I found a strange woman in a cave and I don't know what to do . . .

23

She tried to say it, to tell Uncle Nod, to get his advice. But she couldn't. Again, nothing came. Her tongue seized up, went numb, wouldn't move. A faint gurgling sound came as her words caught in her throat.

Uncle Nod turned. He thought it was a sob, the strange, sad little sound that she made.

'Oh, love,' he sighed.

'It's OK, it's nothing,' Ailsa said, then hurried away.

The house was quiet when she got there. Moxie ran in, glad to be out of the heat. He was panting and he lapped some water from his bowl before slinking off under the kitchen table. Ailsa's mum would still be upstairs. She hadn't left her room since they got here. Aunt Bertha might be up there, making a fuss, making sure she took her medicine, trying to coax some life out of her.

'Oh, boy,' Ailsa sighed to Moxie. The world seemed so strange to her sometimes. She didn't know what to make of any of it.

Four

Mrs Tomlinson lived in the house next to Aunt Bertha and Uncle Nod's. Ailsa met her coming up the garden path as she and Moxie were leaving on a walk. Moxie wagged his tail and Mrs Tomlinson smiled and laughed. She had a double chin and it wobbled.

'You're always on your way out,' she said to Ailsa by way of greeting.

Ailsa shrugged. 'I don't like hanging about,' she said. 'I like to be out, just me and Moxie, you know.'

Ailsa saw that Mrs Tomlinson was carrying a biscuit tin. She had a bag over one shoulder. The tin had a picture of a teddy bear stencilled onto its lid. The bag was woven from lots of different coloured wool.

'I was just coming up to see how your poor ma was doing,' Mrs Tomlinson said.

'Oh, aye,' Ailsa replied.

'And your aunt and uncle, like.'

'Aye.'

'And yourself, of course,' she said. 'How are you holding up, love?'

'Aye.' Ailsa shrugged. She didn't really know what to say and neither did Mrs Tomlinson.

'Well . . .' Mrs Tomlinson began. 'Your ma, then? She OK?'

'You know.' Ailsa shrugged again.

'Of course.'

Mrs Tomlinson pulled the lid off the biscuit tin. It was a little stiff and she had to dig her nails under the rim. She grunted and it came off and she held the open tin forwards, proffering it to Ailsa. There were neat little stacks of chocolate brownies inside.

'I made them for you all, to cheer everyone up a bit,' Mrs Tomlinson said. 'It's not much, but you know.'

Ailsa looked at her.

'I'm sure no one would mind you having one now,' Mrs Tomlinson said. 'Especially not with the amount of trekking to and fro you get up to. You need your energy. Go on.'

'Aye, thank you,' Ailsa said, taking one.

She bit into it. It was chewy and sweet. The middle was soft goo.

Mrs Tomlinson put the lid back on the tin and opened her bag. She showed Ailsa. Inside was a collection of dried, colourful starfish, all red and yellow and orange.

'I found them down at the beach this morning,' Mrs Tomlinson said. 'They looked ever so jolly. I've arranged a few on the sideboard at home. I thought you all might like some.'

'Aye,' Ailsa said. She thought they were horrible. They were dead things and Mrs Tomlinson was treating them like decorations from a shop. But she had known Mrs Tomlinson her whole life and Uncle Nod and Aunt Bertha both thought very highly of her, so she didn't say anything. She just nodded.

Moxie whined.

'Oh, look at me, keeping you from your walkies, blethering on like this,' Mrs Tomlinson said to him. He wagged at her. 'I'll let you get on, then,' she told Ailsa. 'I'll go in and see what's what with your aunt and your ma.'

27

Ailsa and Moxie ran off, leaving Mrs Tomlinson to it. They jogged over to the clifftop paths and then slowed to a walk as Ailsa finished her brownie. She climbed up onto a rocky, mossy outcrop that hung out a little way over the cliffs. The distant harbour was quiet now. A gentle, warm breeze blew past. Staring down below, she followed the long, curling line of coast. She knew that the cave waited, far off, half a mile or so distant and hidden by a great jutting corner of land.

Again, she was drawn to it. Repelled by it, but drawn to it, too. Such sadness came from it, from that strange, strange woman, and Ailsa couldn't stop thinking about her.

Moxie led her down to the cliff path. He kept his head held high. Long, dry grass tickled Ailsa's legs above her wellies. It took them about ten minutes to get to the turn-off they needed, a slim track that took them to the top of the hidden path. They struck downwards, half climbing down some rocks and jumping down a few others.

They came out onto the small strip of beach. Grey stone and coarse sand crunched beneath her feet. Moxie's paws pushed great prints into it. The slab of rock leading up to

28

the cave mouth was largely above the water. The cave itself was as obscured as ever, shadowy and covered in gorse and washed-up seaweed. A couple of newly fallen boulders lay beside the opening, half cracked from their drop.

Ailsa began to tremble. Her stomach tightened and she thought she might throw up Mrs Tomlinson's brownie. Moxie was sure of himself, however. He ran straight up the rocks and into the cave's mouth without a second glance.

Ailsa climbed along the rocks, following Moxie. Her hands shook as she took out her torch. Her skin crawled as she pushed through the wet seaweed and clinging gorse around the cave's mouth. She heard the faint drip and splash of water and the smell hit her, making her gag once more. The cave was cold. The deep chill seemed to seep through her, into her very bones, so different to the summer's warmth outside. It was accompanied by the same aching sadness she had felt the last time she was here. Everywhere was dark. Her torchlight barely seemed able to cut through it and she faltered a few paces in.

Moxie whined, however. His voice was a comfort. It made the cold less potent. It made the sadness less awful.

Ailsa managed to find him with her torch as the light finally made an impact.

He was by the rock pool, which was as she remembered it. She thought that she and Moxie were alone. She thought the strange woman was gone, or that she had imagined her in the first place, or any number of things. She thought she wouldn't see her again.

She was wrong. Moxie panted and wagged his tail. The strange woman was there, half in the water, half out, and slumped over, seemingly asleep.

Her skin was as pallid as it had been before. It looked raw in places. Sores covered her arms and made her look like she was decomposing. Her cheeks were sunken and an air of decay surrounded her.

'You're back then . . .' the strange woman croaked in her coarse voice. Her eyes flickered open, and Ailsa jumped backwards.

The strange woman sounded like it was a lot of effort to speak. It seemed a lot of effort for her just to look at Ailsa.

'Who-who are you?' Ailsa stuttered.

'Ha!' The woman's laughter sounded empty.

'What are you doing here?' Ailsa asked.

'Not much . . .' the strange woman replied. 'Doesn't look like I get up to anything . . . does it?' She sighed and slid a little further into the water. Her chest heaved and then sagged.

'Aren't you cold in there?' Ailsa said. 'You're not wearing a thing!'

'I don't feel a thing . . . more's the pity,' the strange woman said.

'How did you get here?' Ailsa asked.

The strange woman sighed once again and turned her face away from Ailsa.

'I . . . I can get you out of here,' Ailsa said. Her voice trembled, nearly snuffed out even as she spoke. She realised how scared she was, how desperate. She was confused, too. What on earth should she make of this strange woman?

However, despite the fear, despite the confusion, she wanted to help. She wanted to do something. So she took a deep breath and tried to put everything else aside for the moment.

'I can help you,' she told the strange woman. 'Aren't you scared the sea will come in and sweep you away or something?'

'It hasn't so far . . . though it could very well try,' the strange woman whispered.

Moxie whined and yipped, and she rolled her eyes to look at him without moving her head.

'Same to you . . . *glodhund*,' she said in her tired voice. Her chest sagged again.

'You going to stand there gawping all day?' she asked Ailsa.

Odd, faint lights played just underneath the rock pool's surface. They seemed to shimmer across the strange woman's skin. Her outline blurred slightly as it glimmered, as though it wasn't really there, as though it had been conjured from the light and the water itself.

'I don't understand,' said Ailsa.

'Few would . . . Few do . . .' the strange woman whispered.

'Can't you leave? How long have you been here?'

'Enough, little one,' the strange woman said. She said it quietly, but Ailsa clamped her mouth tightly shut. 'Too much . . . too many questions . . .'

The odd lights grew darker. They grew sickly as the strange woman spoke.

Ailsa's heart pounded. The sadness threatened to swallow her. The smell of brine and decay stung her nose. Looking closer, she could see strange patches on the woman's skin. There were scaled patches around the sores. They were blistered and raw. They looked like they were weeping. She saw pieces of seaweed next to the strange woman. They were chewed up with bite marks on them, like they had been half eaten.

'You can't stay here,' Ailsa finally managed to say.

'Foolish child . . .' the strange woman said. Her voice was growing fainter.

'But you can't.'

'Go away!'

'That's rude,' Ailsa said, frowning.

'You'll hear ruder . . . if you're not careful . . . Now go. Go!'

'Can I come back?'

'Do what you want . . .' the woman said.

'Can I bring you anything?'

The strange woman was silent for a long minute. Then she cackled emptily again. 'Cocoa . . . and sugar,' she whispered.

'Pardon?'

'Cocoa and sugar . . . like the sailors of old used to carry . . . between the worlds . . .'

'OK.'

'Cocoa and sugar . . .' The strange woman was only half conscious by now, exhausted by the conversation. A line of drool escaped her mouth. It hung for a second, then dropped into the rock pool's water. 'Now . . . go away . . . !' she finally croaked.

Ailsa backed away from the rock pool and the strange woman. When she had taken a couple of steps, her courage gave out. She turned on the spot and ran and kept running until she was outside the cave, up the path, and out on the clifftops. There, she finally stopped and caught her breath, shaking.

She brushed pieces of seaweed and chunks of gorse from her T-shirt and shorts, and from Moxie's fur. They both stood blinking in the sunshine.

She stood there for a while. The tides crashed on the beach below. They crashed all around the cave. Her heart rate slowed down. Her breathing grew steady. Then her fear turned into concern, into worry for the strange woman.

'She isn't just a strange woman,' Ailsa whispered, half to Moxie, half to herself.

If she was, someone would have done something. Or else she might have died a long time ago, for there was no doubt in Ailsa's mind that she had been there for a long time. Ailsa couldn't just ring the police or call an ambulance or any of the usual things that grown-ups told her to do in emergencies like this.

'I don't think she's normal,' she told Moxie. 'She's magical, or something. Don't you think?'

Moxie barked and wagged his tail. He bobbed his head and it looked to Ailsa as though he were nodding.

She realised that she wanted to help the strange woman, if she could.

'At least I can try to help someone,' she muttered as they turned to go.

Five

'You're Bertha and Nod's niece, then?' a voice asked.

Ailsa turned around. She was walking home past the high walls of the Galach house. A girl was peering over the top. She was maybe a year older than Ailsa and she had dark hair and wide eyes that shone.

'You're Bertha and Nod's niece?' the girl asked again. 'I've seen you around before. Maybe last year. I don't know. I'm usually away at school. I'm Camilla. Galach, that is. Camilla Galach.'

Ailsa nodded. 'I'm Ailsa,' she said.

'Ailsa,' Camilla repeated. 'That's a very pretty name.'

'Aye?'

'Yes. Yes, it is.'

'OK, then.' Ailsa blushed a little. She didn't really know what to say to that.

'Are you here for the summer?' Camilla asked.

'Aye.'

'The whole summer?'

'Aye,' Ailsa said. 'I think so.'

Camilla's head disappeared back down behind the wall. 'Wonderful,' her voice called over it. 'Lovely to meet you, Ailsa.'

Uncle Nod was clattering around the kitchen when Ailsa got home. His clothes were splattered in paint. There was a smudge of it on his nose and some matted into one of his bushy eyebrows.

'Good day?' he asked.

'Aye.'

'Up to much?'

Ailsa shook her head. She could barely begin to think about it.

'Just out with Moxie,' she said. 'Along the shore, like.'

'You mind the tides?'

'Aye.'

'Good girl.' Uncle Nod moved around a bit more, rifling through a couple of drawers. 'I saw you chatting to the Galach girl, there.'

37

'Aye.'

'Well, then,' he said, and continued his search.

'I've told you about the Galachs before, haven't I?' he asked.

'Aye,' Ailsa said. 'You told me they're gangsters. That nobody likes them, but everyone's scared of them.'

'Aye,' Uncle Nod said. 'That just about sums it up.'

He had a packet of half-frozen bacon in one hand. He found a small knife and began to trim slices from it, cutting through a thin layer of ice. He pulled one away and threw it into the air. Moxie leaped up and caught it, then ran off into the other room.

'Fry-up, tonight,' he told Ailsa. 'Bit of a treat, like.'

'Aye,' she said. 'That'll be nice.' She sat at the kitchen table to watch him work. 'Has Mum eaten today?' she asked.

'Aye, a bit,' Uncle Nod sighed. 'Though not as much as I'd like.'

'Aye,' Aunt Bertha said, coming into the kitchen. She had a jug of flowers in her hands that she set down on a sideboard.

Ailsa noticed that a couple of Mrs Tomlinson's dried starfish lay on the sideboard too, all oranges and faded reds. She still thought they looked horrible, but she didn't say anything.

'Your mum had some sweet tea this morning,' Aunt Bertha told Ailsa. 'And I got her to eat a spot of toast for her lunch.'

Ailsa nodded. That was good, she thought. 'Maybe she can have some brownies later,' she said.

'Who said anything about any brownies?' Uncle Nod asked. He flipped some bacon and then cracked a couple of eggs into the pan. He tipped a can of baked beans into a pot and lit the ring beneath it.

'I saw Mrs Tomlinson when I left earlier,' Ailsa said. 'She gave me one. It was nice.'

'Oh, aye? Well, then, fair enough,' Uncle Nod said. A few slices of toast popped up out of the toaster and he began to spread butter onto them. 'The amount you've been tramping up and down those cliffs, I dare say you need the extra energy.'

'Aye, Mrs Tomlinson said the same thing.'

Uncle Nod chuckled. Then he looked sombre. 'I'm not sure your mum would go for them though, my love. The brownies, like.'

39

'Aye, maybe not.'

They all helped themselves after dinner, though. Uncle Nod got the biscuit tin from Mrs Tomlinson out and left it on the table. Ailsa ate one. Then she sneaked a couple of extra ones when nobody else was looking, wrapping them up in a tissue.

She went into her mum's room to see if she wanted one, but she was sleeping. Her skin was pale. Her chest moved only lightly.

'Maybe tomorrow,' Ailsa whispered.

She placed the brownies on her mum's bedside table and then sat at the end of her bed. The evening was bright outside. A sliver of light cut through the crack in the curtains. It played on motes of dust, spinning in the air.

They are falling, scattering, without anything to hold them up, Ailsa thought as she watched them. She looked at her mum.

I'm falling, without you to hold me up, she thought.

'Oh, Mum,' she whispered. 'I don't know how to help you.'

I met a strange woman in a cave. I spoke to her.

40

She couldn't say the words, still. She wasn't sure if she would ever be able to.

'But I can help her, I think,' she whispered to her mum. 'And I think she's got no one else. No one at all.'

Ailsa's dreams were turbulent once more. Her mum drowned in them, and then Ailsa herself began to drown. The cliffs all around began to crumble. The Galach house fell into the sea and then Uncle Nod and Aunt Bertha's house began to fall in on itself. Then she became her mum and drowned as her. Fishes with long legs and sharp teeth grabbed at her. Then they ran ashore, looking for people to eat.

She woke up gasping. Again, she thought that she had drowned for real. Again, it was cold sweat and clinging sheets and nothing more.

Night still lay heavy outside her window. The moon was nearly full, though, and the sky was clear of clouds. Silver moonlight coated everything, and a thousand twinkling stars added their own distant glow. She felt something out there pulling at her, and she sighed.

The house shook as Uncle Nod snored in the room next door. Ailsa padded out of her own room and into her mum's. Everything was still and silent in there. She stood watching her mum as she slept. The fishermen would be up and about their business in a few hours. Then the birds would begin to sing the dawn chorus. Ailsa doubted the song would reach in here.

She wrapped up warm in a jumper and jacket and pulled her wellies on. Moxie came trotting sleepily to her side and nuzzled into her.

'I've got to go and see her, the strange woman,' Ailsa told him. 'You can't come.'

Moxie began to whine in the back of his throat. He began to growl.

'OK, OK,' she said. 'But you've got to be quiet. I'm serious.'

Moxie's whining stopped. He wagged his tail and came to stand at heel, silent.

Ailsa put the wrapped-up brownies in her pocket. She took her torch with her as she left the house. It stayed unlit until they reached the cliff path. She didn't want anyone to see them. The silvery light from the moon and the stars clung to everything though, so she could see quite clearly. A deep silence came with the light, broken only by the surf's lulling far below. Moxie glided like a ghost beside her.

She was terrified. She was glad Moxie was there, after all, but she still jumped at every shadow. Every time a cloud passed over the moon or a bush rustled or anything else moved, she gasped. The temptation to turn around and go home nearly caught up with her a couple of times.

'But the strange woman needs help,' she said to Moxie.

She lit the torch when they got to the cliffs. She began to jog along, not wanting to be any longer than she had to be, not wanting to be missed. Moxie ran along quite happily, sometimes alongside her, sometimes pulling ahead. They were both panting hard by the time they reached the cave.

Ailsa hesitated as she stood outside the cave mouth. 'I must be mad,' she whispered to herself. She shivered badly. The wind blew and made her jump. Darkness loomed within. 'I don't think I can go in,' she whispered to Moxie.

Moxie nudged her towards the cave's mouth. Then he ran in himself.

'Moxie!' Ailsa hissed, but it was no good. He was gone.

She hurried in after him.

Bitter coldness met her inside. The sadness was palpable, as ever. It crept over her skin, pricking her with goosebumps. She shone the torch around and a few shadows flickered, looming out at her. The rock pool at the cave's far end seemed to glow faintly, even when she wasn't running the torchlight over it.

The strange woman was up to her chest in the water. Her head hung back and to one side, limp and weak, as though it were too heavy for her own neck to support. Moxie ran over to her, paddling his paws at the water's edge and wagging his tail. He crept as close as he could and gave the strange woman a lick before settling down.

'Foolish *glodhund*,' the strange woman cursed, though she made no move to shoo Moxie away. She looked up at Ailsa instead, struggling to raise her head.

'I thought . . . I told you . . . to go away . . .' she said to Ailsa.

'Yes, you – you did. And I did,' Ailsa replied.

'But you didn't stay away . . .'

Ailsa fumbled the wrapped-up brownies out of her jacket pocket. Her fingers were stiff with the cold. They

44

trembled. Her breath came shallow and misted around her face.

'I-I brought what you asked me to,' Ailsa said.

'What?' the strange woman snapped.

'Cocoa and sugar,' Ailsa said. 'That's right, isn't it? I thought you could do with it.'

The strange woman opened her mouth but said nothing. Ailsa saw that her teeth were like needles. It looked like each one had been filed down to a point. Her tongue licked dry, cracked lips as she glared up at Ailsa.

'Like the sailors of old used to carry,' she said.

'Aye, like you said,' Ailsa replied.

'Why?' The strange woman was guarded. Her eyes were like flint. 'Why . . . why would you do that?'

Ailsa shrugged. 'I don't know. But you're meant to help people, aren't you? And I thought you could do with help. Aunt Bertha and Uncle Nod would go crazy if they knew I was here.'

'Are they your guardians?' the strange woman asked.

'I guess so.'

'No mamma . . . no pappa . . . ?'

'There's my mum,' Ailsa said. 'But she's not well.'

'Who is . . . in this world?' the strange woman whispered. She raised her hands. They shook as they emerged from the water. Her knuckles were split. Dirty talons curled out from her fingertips.

'What are you . . . ?' Ailsa began, but she caught herself.

The strange woman cackled without mirth. It was a dry, wicked sound.

Ailsa tried again. '*Who* are you?' she asked.

'Nothing and nobody,' the woman snapped. 'Not to you or . . . any other *tosk*. Dimwit. Fool . . . Just a memory . . . and not much of one . . . at that.'

The strange woman's mouth ran dry as she spoke. She tried to cup some water in her hands to drink, but she was too weak to lift them to her mouth.

'Here,' Ailsa said. She moved closer, her fear forgotten for the moment, and plunged her own hands into the water. It was so cold that it hurt. It felt like her bones would break with it. But she cupped her palms and lifted some of it to the strange woman's mouth.

The strange woman's lips were like sandpaper, and she made horrible slurping sounds as she drank, but she managed to take a few mouthfuls in.

'I thought saltwater wasn't to drink,' Ailsa said, but the strange woman cut her off with a look.

'Now the cocoa . . . now the . . . sugar . . .' she whispered.

Ailsa took one of the brownies from the paper and held it out. She fed it to the strange woman, who took fast, brutal bites. The brown cake clung to her sharp teeth. She sighed and closed her eyes and lay her head back as she chewed.

'Like it always was . . .' she whispered. '*Vakker* . . . beautiful . . .

'Now . . .' the strange woman hissed. Her voice was sharp. It bounced around the cave.

Ailsa jumped and Moxie ran to her side.

'. . . go away,' the strange woman said, her eyes still closed, her head still back.

Ailsa set the remaining brownie down beside the pool for the strange woman to eat later and backed away. Then, when she had gone a couple of steps, she turned and ran out of the cave with Moxie at her side.

Six

Ailsa saw Camilla Galach again the following day.

She was helping Uncle Nod to carry some of his tools along the lane to his truck. The sun above was beating down with its warmth and the air was thick. Moxie walked half ragged beside them, panting with the heat.

'Daft old thing,' Uncle Nod said, watching Moxie following them. He often said it. Aunt Bertha often asked him if he was talking about the dog or himself. 'Both,' he would reply. 'We're both as old and daft as each other, I'd say.' His eyes would twinkle, and Aunt Bertha would laugh. It was something of a ritual between them. They were both about fifteen years older than Ailsa's mum, but they laughed like children all the time.

Moxie barked up at a tree. The tree was in the Galachs'

garden, looming over the high wall. Camilla was up there, curled up in its highest boughs. A hardback book rested across her knees. She seemed to be thoroughly engrossed in it, until Moxie barked a second time.

'Moxie!' Uncle Nod snapped, as Camilla jumped. She nearly dropped her book. 'Sorry, lass,' Uncle Nod called up to her.

'It's OK, Nod!' Camilla called back brightly. 'Hello, again, Ailsa,' she said, smiling.

'Hi,' Ailsa replied.

They all stood in silence for a few seconds.

Then Uncle Nod grunted. 'I can make it the rest of the way by myself,' he told Ailsa. He tucked the box he was carrying under one armpit and took the small box in Ailsa's hands from her, then headed off to his truck.

'I've been reading all day,' Camilla said. She didn't raise her voice very much, but it still managed to carry well enough down the tree and over the wall.

'Aye?' Ailsa asked, looking at the book. 'What's that, then?'

Camilla held her book up. A picture of a couple of men in horned helmets took up the front cover.

'It's an old book of my grandfather's,' Camilla said. 'They're all Norse myths. You know, Vikings. My grandfather was obsessed with them. He left a whole box of books up in the loft. No one else is into it, but I love them.'

'Oh, aye.'

'I've been reading lots of them this summer. I was just reading about Yggdrasil, the World Tree,' she said.

'What's that?' Ailsa asked.

'A giant tree at the centre of the Vikings' universe. Its roots connect all the different worlds together.'

'Aye?'

'Yes. And Yggdrasil's branches reach right up into the heavens. The Norse gods visit it every day. It has three roots that connect it to different places and lots of magical creatures live in it. The wellbeing of everything depends on it. When the tree shakes, it heralds the arrival of Ragnarok, the end of the world!' She shook the tree she was in. Leaves fell down and she giggled.

Ailsa smiled.

A voice called from within the Galach house and Camilla looked around.

'I've got to go, now,' she said. 'I'll see you later, Ailsa.'

'Aye, then,' Ailsa said, but Camilla was already gone, dropping nimbly out of the tree and behind the wall.

Ailsa took Moxie out walking in the hills later that afternoon, where the sun blazed and the skies were wide and open, and she could get away from the fuss of other folks. Below, in the distance, she could see blue water lapping at the shores. She began to sweat a little before long, and Moxie had his tongue lolling from his mouth. He looked weary as they climbed a particularly steep slope to the summit of one of the highest hills.

'Wow, boy,' she panted, staring out.

The view swept around them. Miles opened up before Ailsa. She spread her arms wide, feeling free. She never felt free in the city, at home. She never felt free when her mum got sick and it was just them. She only ever really felt free when they came to visit Uncle Nod and Aunt Bertha, when she and Moxie could go off together like this and get lost in the island's wild places.

There was a deep crater on the hill's opposite side, carved from a chunk of grassy rock that jutted out over

51

the valley below. A brook carved its way around the hill. It looked like it would usually be a heavy stream churning down from the heights, but it had turned to a trickle in the sunshine's dense heat. A wide pool sat in the crater, diminished yet still fulsome enough. Slick, flat stones that looked like they would usually be underwater lay on its banks, soaking up the day.

Ailsa and Moxie ran over to it. Moxie plunged in up to his neck and sent water spraying with his hard wag and heavy movements. Ailsa followed, pulling off her wellies and socks and paddling in up to the hem of her shorts. Moxie pranced all about, splashing Ailsa. Then, laughing, she slipped over and landed bodily in the water with a great splash.

The water was warm from the day. It was crystal clear and fresh, unlike the sea's brine. She wallowed in it, lying on her back, closing her eyes and half floating, feeling it touching her skin. A faint breeze rippled it and she breathed it in, relishing it.

Moxie panted beside her. When she climbed out, dripping, a quarter of an hour or so later, he stuck firmly to her. He licked her mercilessly, lapping up all the water from her hair and clothes. Then they sat together, drying in the sun as wisps of cloud scudded overhead and all around hummed with the heady peace of a midsummer day.

Ailsa was red raw from the sun by the time she got home. Her skin felt tight and sore. Her face felt stretched by it. She was sweating once more and the sweat stung as it ran in rivulets down her cheeks.

'Oh, Ailsa, by the heavens!' Uncle Nod exclaimed as she trudged into the kitchen.

Dr Arbuthnot's jacket was over the back of one of the dining chairs and Ailsa could hear footsteps and hushed voices coming from upstairs.

'I thought I told you to put sun cream on!' Uncle Nod said. He came over to fuss at her, kneeling down and peering at her skin. 'And I told you to take it with you. Reapply it every couple of hours, I said! Good grief, my love.'

'Aye, I did,' Ailsa said.

'Well, look at you!'

'Aye.'

'It's like it washed off. Were you down at the seashore?'

'No, up in the hills. We went into a pool.'

'Foolish girl,' he muttered. 'Well, sit yourself down, then. Let's see to it.'

If anything, Ailsa's skin darkened as Uncle Nod told her off. Beneath the hard, shiny red skin of her burn, she began to blush furiously. She was embarrassed and guilty. She should have remembered to put more cream on when she came out of the pool.

He disappeared and returned a few minutes later with a large bottle of lotion. He began to rub it all over her arms and shoulders. She winced as it went on. Uncle Nod's hands were strong and calloused and her burned skin was delicate. He squeezed some of the cream into her hands and she applied it gingerly to her cheeks.

'You put some more on before bed,' he told her.

'Aye, Uncle Nod,' she said.

'And again in the morning, like.'

'Aye.'

They sat across from one another. Uncle Nod got up to pour her a cup of tea. Ailsa sat blowing it as he stared idly out of the window. He saw her eyeing Dr Arbuthnot's jacket at one point.

'Aye,' he sighed. He leaned forwards. 'You OK, love?'

She nodded.

'Aye, but, you know,' Uncle Nod said. He rolled his eyes at the jacket and then up at the ceiling, from where she could hear a couple of sets of footsteps moving about.

'Aye,' Ailsa said.

'Pretty strong stuff, all of this,' Uncle Nod said.

'Aye.'

Ailsa's eyes began to sting, and she realised that they were prickling with tears.

Uncle Nod reached over and put one of his big, rough hands over her own.

'Your ma's always been tough,' he said. 'But she's also always been kind of delicate too, you know? If that makes any sense?'

Ailsa shrugged and Uncle Nod sighed.

'I was always rubbish with words,' he muttered. 'But . . . listen. You know I'm a lot older than your ma, right? I was already older than you are now when she was born. And suddenly, I had this wee sister.'

'Aye, I know,' Ailsa said.

'You'll also know that her birth nearly finished off both your ma and your grandma. It was difficult. I'll never forget it.'

Ailsa nodded. She had heard the story often enough.

'Aye, but it didn't finish them off, did it?' Uncle Nod carried on. 'They were both at death's door, but they never gave in. Neither of them. Your grandma carried on another twenty years or more. And your ma's always been one of the strongest people I've ever known. Real iron in her blood, you know?'

'Aye,' Ailsa whispered. She was surprised to see tears appear in her uncle's eyes. His voice shook a little.

'She fights and she fights,' he said. 'And she'll keep on fighting, you'll see. She'll fight whatever this is, and she'll fight whatever comes after that. She'll come out the other end swinging. She's strong.'

'Aye, Uncle Nod,' Ailsa whispered. She squeezed his hand. 'I know.'

Dr Arbuthnot left a little while later. He and Aunt Bertha came downstairs, and Aunt Bertha fussed over Ailsa's sunburn almost as badly as Uncle Nod had. She put more cream on and Dr Arbuthnot frowned at Ailsa, disapproving, before taking his jacket and heading out.

Ailsa went up to see her mum after dinner. The curtains were open a crack in her room and sunlight spilled in, a hazy, dusty ray that cut through everything else. It was cold in there, however, and Ailsa's mum was tucked up in bed. The sheets were neat and straight, but her mum's hair was bedraggled. It looked lank and straggly. A couple of half empty pill bottles sat at her bedside, locked in a plastic box.

'Mum?' she whispered. 'Mum?' she repeated, a little louder. Her mum stirred ever so slightly. Ailsa crept up to the bedside.

Her mum's skin was pale. Ailsa touched one hand to her cheek. It was cold and clammy where Ailsa's skin was sun-scorched, warm and bright.

'Love?' Ailsa's mum whispered. She half opened her eyes and looked up at Ailsa. There was no expression on her face and her eyes were unfocussed.

I met a strange woman in a cave and I went back to see her and took her sugar and cocoa . . . I think I'm going mad . . . I don't know what to do . . .

The words didn't come. Of course they didn't.

'You get better, now, Mum,' Ailsa whispered. It was all she could manage.

Moxie was waiting for her outside. He nuzzled her hand as she tiptoed out of her mum's room and they both went off to sit on her own bed together. The whole house was quiet.

Seven

Ailsa woke up in the night. Her sheets were pressing against her, hot and heavy. Everything itched. Everything burned. She tried to scratch her face when she was only half awake. It felt like needles pressing into her flesh as soon as she touched it. Yowling, she sat bolt upright, suddenly fully awake.

Her heart beat fast. Her skin throbbed. It felt like it was on fire, like it was bursting from the inside with the sunburn.

She closed her eyes. She breathed deeply and tried to fight the pain, but it didn't go away. Instead, cold tears began to well in her eyes. They clung to her lower eyelashes, built up, and then began to drip down her cheeks.

It was no good. She needed ... something. Help, maybe. Support, maybe. Just someone to do something.

She got up and padded over to her door. Even her joints hurt. They were throbbing.

Going outside into the hallway, she knocked softly on Uncle Nod and Aunt Bertha's door. Uncle Nod's snores drowned out all other sound. They sawed through the house, rumbling and roaring.

Ailsa knocked a little louder. Moxie came trotting out behind her, half asleep and curious.

She pushed the door open and peered into the darkness.

'Aunt Bertha,' she whispered. 'Aunt Bertha!'

The darkness faded a little. Ailsa could see two lumpy shapes on a double bed. One of them began to stir, sitting up.

'Aye, love,' Aunt Bertha mumbled. She squinted at Ailsa, bleary eyes. 'You OK?'

'It's my skin . . .'

'Aye.'

'It's on fire.'

'Come on, then.'

Aunt Bertha heaved herself out of bed. Her footsteps were heavy as she blundered over to the door.

'Not to worry, love,' she told Ailsa as they both headed into the hallway. 'We'll see you right.'

Aunt Bertha gestured to the bathroom and they both shut themselves inside.

First, she gave Ailsa a couple of painkillers from the bathroom cabinet.

'Just to cut through the worst of it,' she said.

Ailsa cupped some water from the sink in her hands and swilled it back, swallowing the pills.

Then Aunt Bertha got some lotion out of the cabinet.

'Take your things off, then, love,' she said.

Ailsa stripped down. Her skin hurt as she slid her pyjamas off, but the cool night air felt good as she stood there. It soothed her a little.

Aunt Bertha's hands were rough and calloused, just like Uncle Nod's. They were gentler, though. Aunt Bertha was gentler. She squeezed a good dollop of lotion into her palm, rubbed her hands together, then very tenderly began to rub it into Ailsa's skin.

It burned. It hurt. Every touch felt like it was going through her. However, the lotion's coldness mixed with the chill night air. It softened the pain. Aunt Bertha put more and more on. She stuck her tongue out the corner of her mouth as she worked. She caught Ailsa's eye at one point and winked.

'The sun's a harsh master, my ma used to say,' she told Ailsa. 'It keeps us true. It keeps us alive. But it can burn us, too.

'Never mind, though,' she said, finishing up and putting the lid back on the lotion bottle. Ailsa's skin felt a lot better. 'There's no damage done that can't be undone.'

'Aye, Aunt Bertha,' Ailsa said. 'Thank you.'

'Now, off to bed,' Aunt Bertha said. 'Get some sleep. That's where the real healing happens.'

'You caught the sun,' Camilla said the following afternoon. She was in front of the high, wrought iron gates that led into her house.

'It looks like you've been crying, too,' Camilla added.

Ailsa had been. She shrugged, then winced with the pain from her sore joints.

'What's up?' Camilla asked.

'My mum,' Ailsa told her. 'She's sick, you know.'

'Yes,' Camilla said. She nodded and frowned.

'It feels like she's never going to get out of that bed,' Ailsa said.

Camilla sighed. 'Has anyone shown you around?' she asked.

Ailsa shook her head. 'I know the area. Aunt Bertha and Uncle Nod have always lived here. And I've always come to visit them.'

'I bet there's stuff you haven't seen,' Camilla retorted. She smiled and her eyes twinkled.

Ailsa shrugged. 'Probably. There's lots I've not seen. I bet there's lots that lots of people haven't seen.'

'Come on,' Camilla said. 'Let me take you to a secret place. I bet it will cheer you up.'

Camilla took Ailsa's hand and began to drag her up the road. They took a slim turning into a small lane. They began to run along lightly, Camilla leading, Ailsa following.

The lane was lined with tall trees and high walls made from jagged stones all stacked together. A stile sat at its end. Camilla let go of Ailsa's hand, vaulted over it, and beckoned for Ailsa to follow. It emerged onto a small patch of woodland, which in turn opened up to a long finger of grassy clifftop jutting out into the sea. There was an old lighthouse way out at the end and a slender strip of beach hidden down a slope, completely obscured by the finger.

'Wow,' Ailsa said. 'It's beautiful.'

'I know, right?' Camilla said, standing at the top of the slope down to it. 'A hidden piece of paradise. Come on!'

Camilla took Ailsa's hand again. She led her down to the beach, scrabbling a bit on the steep scree. She took off her shoes and socks at the bottom of the slope. She took off her shorts and left everything in a pile. Then she laughed and ran out across the sand and into the sea.

'It's lovely and cool!' she called back to Ailsa.

Ailsa took off her own shoes and socks. She took off her shorts and jogged out to the water. It lapped at her feet and ankles. It splashed up to her shins and made her gasp with its deep coldness. It hurt her when it splashed up over her torso. The salt seemed to eat into her sunburn, chewing at her, stinging like crazy. But it was fun. She felt free.

Camilla laughed, bent over, scooped some water and splashed Ailsa. She danced and splashed, and Ailsa was soon laughing along with her. Thoughts of her mother and her sunburn disappeared for the moment. Thoughts of the strange woman disappeared, too.

They sat on the sand, afterwards. The sun bathed everything in an orange glow as it began to dip to the horizon. Ailsa kept herself in the finger's shadow. Her skin still really hurt. It felt tight and raw, and she didn't want it getting any worse. However, the cool of the shade was nice. A gentle breeze blew and soothed the burning.

Camilla stretched out on a flat slab of rock in the full sunshine.

'My mum used to love the seaside,' Ailsa said after a while. 'Well, she sort of still does, I guess. She will, you know, when she gets over this. If it doesn't change her too much.'

She caught Camilla looking at her, worried, a little confused.

'It never really changes her, though,' she said. 'You know, her being ill and all that. She comes around again and she's like she always was. So she'll love the seaside again, I reckon.'

'Did you used to go a lot?' Camilla asked.

'Aye. Out here, when we came to stay for the summers.

And on holiday, sometimes, a couple of times. We've flown a couple of times. Been to Spain and that. Mum taught me to bodyboard one time. I wanted to surf, standing up properly, you know? But Mum said it takes ages to learn. She said we should start with bodyboarding, then go on to surf another time, if I still wanted to.'

'And did you?'

Ailsa shrugged. 'Never really got the chance. We never went back on holiday after that. But bodyboarding was great. Mum showed me how to stand and wait for the waves, how to jump on the board and catch the surf, how to ride it all the way back to the beach.'

'Were you any good?' Camilla asked.

'Mum was better than me to start with,' Ailsa replied. 'Then we spent pretty much every day of our holiday at the beach, in the sea. We didn't do any of the other stuff we'd planned before we went, just spent our whole time bodyboarding. I was as good as her at the end, maybe better, even. It was the best week ever.'

'I've done it a few times,' Camilla said. 'And wind-surfing, and kayaking.'

'What's that?'

'Kayaking? Kayaks are little boats, sort of like one-person canoes.'

'Aye, that'd be good,' Ailsa said. 'I always love going out on Uncle Nod's rowing boat.'

Camilla smiled at her. An orange sun began to set before them, turning the whole sky ruddy, pink and golden.

'Why haven't I seen you before?' Ailsa asked. 'I come to the island lots, but we've never met.'

Camilla shrugged.

'I'm usually away,' she said. 'You know, school during term. It's a very good one, my school.'

'Aye?'

'Yes. It's private.'

'Oh.'

'That means my daddy pays for me to go.'

'Why?' Ailsa asked. Her mum didn't have to pay for her to go to school.

'Because Daddy says private schools are better,' Camilla said.

Ailsa still didn't understand. She didn't agree. Her school was just as good as any, no matter if anyone was foolish enough to pay to go to theirs. But Camilla didn't seem about to offer any more explanation.

'And it's a boarding school,' Camilla said.

'What does that mean?'

'It means I live there.'

'But you live here,' Ailsa said.

'No, I live at school, except during the holidays.'

'Don't your parents miss you?'

'No.'

'Don't you miss them?'

Camilla shrugged.

'Aye, well then,' Ailsa said. She didn't really understand. 'What about the holidays? Why haven't I seen you over the summer before?'

'I'm at summer school, usually,' Camilla replied. 'I've been to ones all over the world. My parents send me so that they don't have to put up with me, I think. But this year, my summer school was cancelled. So I'm here, instead.'

Camilla breathed deeply and smiled, though Ailsa could see she was sad. It was in her eyes. Before she could say anything more, though, Camilla pointed at the lighthouse at the end of the finger.

'Look,' she said. 'It's been abandoned for years. The light still works. It's automated. It comes on by itself every night. The coastguard sends people out for maintenance every few months, but the house itself is empty. No need for a lighthouse keeper these days. I used to love it when I was a small child. My Grandpa Peter would take me out sailing and I'd always stare at it as we went past.'

Ailsa craned her neck and saw what looked like a cluster of cottages and outhouses nestled into the lighthouse's base.

'Dad just bought it a few weeks ago. It's massive and there are a few smaller buildings around it, see. He's going to turn it into a hotel,' Camilla said.

'Why?'

Camilla shrugged. 'So people can come and stay. He says he'll make a fortune off people coming from the mainland every summer.'

'Oh,' Ailsa said. 'Aye, he's probably right. Folks always want out of the city where I live. And Uncle Nod's forever fixing up pleasure boats for the tourists to row. There's enough of them.'

Camilla shrugged again. 'My daddy's smart. He's a really smart businessman, just nobody ever appreciates it.

Everyone calls him a gangster,' she said. 'I've heard them, behind my back, thinking I don't know what they're talking about. And I don't know if he is or not. But either way, he's smart.'

A great ruckus lifted up above them. Hundreds of birds emerged from cracks in the finger, billowing out in a massive cloud. The sound of tiny wings beating broke the air. The cloud billowed and banked before rising up to fly in front of the sun.

'They're terns, I think,' Camilla said.

'Look at that,' Ailsa said, pointing. A couple of very large, black birds sat on a rock, watching the billowing terns.

'Huginn and Muninn,' Camilla said.

'What?' Ailsa asked.

'Two ravens, sitting there,' Camilla said. 'Huginn and Muninn were Odin's ravens. Odin was the king of the gods, and they were his messengers. I read it in one of my grandfather's books.'

They walked back together as the sun began to set. The two ravens watched them as they climbed the scree back up onto the finger. Though she and Ailsa had been chatting away happily all afternoon, Camilla began to fall quiet as they drew closer to home. She was completely silent as they got to the end of the lane.

She turned to Ailsa as they were about to step out onto the road. Her eyes were large. They held Ailsa still. 'Could we do something like this again?' she asked. 'If . . . if, you know, you want to, and you're around this summer.'

'Aye,' Ailsa said. She nodded. 'I'd like that.'

'Good, then,' Camilla said. She turned and ran back to her house, leaving Ailsa to walk the last short while back to Aunt Bertha and Uncle Nod's on her own.

Moxie came charging up to her as she got to the front garden. Aunt Bertha was there, cleaning some large paint brushes in a bucket of turpentine.

'That one's been going spare with you away for the afternoon,' she told Ailsa by way of greeting, nodding at Moxie. 'Daft old fool.'

'Aye.'

Ailsa crouched down. Moxie nuzzled at her, wagging his tail and licking at her face. His tongue hurt her tender skin, but it tickled too. She laughed and pushed him away, then pulled him close to tickle him under his chin.

71

'Where have you been?' Aunt Bertha asked as Ailsa continued to stroke Moxie.

'Just down at the seafront with Camilla.'

'Galach?' Aunt Bertha asked, raising an eyebrow.

Ailsa nodded and Aunt Bertha frowned. 'Well then,' she said. 'I hope you stayed out of the sun.'

'Aye, I stayed in the shade mostly,' Ailsa said. 'And I put on plenty of cream.'

'Good. Now, on you go,' Aunt Bertha said. 'Get yourself inside and washed up. Your uncle's got some supper waiting for you, hen.'

'Aye, Aunt Bertha.'

Eight

Ailsa and Moxie went back down to the cave the following morning. They saw Camilla as they passed the Galach house. She was sitting up high on the wall, dangling her legs down. A new book lay open across her knees. Her shins were red with the sun, though nowhere near as bad as Ailsa's own skin. It looked sore, but not painful like Ailsa's. A broad brimmed hat flopped over her head and down to her shoulders at the back.

'Hi,' Ailsa said.

'Oh, hi,' Camilla called back down, a little startled. She had been in her own world, completely engrossed, Ailsa thought.

'What's that you've got?' she asked, nodding at Camilla's book.

'I'm reading about the ravens.'

'The ones you told me about?'

'Huginn and Muninn, yes.'

'The god's messengers?'

Camilla nodded.

Ailsa looked at the cover of Camilla's book. It had a picture of a man with one eye, dressed in faded red, with a helmet on his head and a big bushy beard. Two birds sat on his shoulders, and he held a spear in one hand.

'Is that the god?' Ailsa asked.

Camilla nodded. 'Odin, the Allfather, king of the old gods.'

'With his ravens.'

'Yes,' Camilla said.

'They look like they're talking to him,' Ailsa said.

'That's because they are,' Camilla replied. 'Odin granted them the power of speech.'

'Oh.'

'They fly all over, looking and listening. Watching everyone,' Camilla said. 'Then they bring the news back to Odin. That way, Odin knows everything that's going on.'

A bird flew overhead as Camilla spoke. Ailsa jumped

and looked up as Moxie stood on his hind legs and snapped at the air. It was only a gull, though, gliding out towards the sea. It carried on over the cliffs and off to the horizon.

'Odin also had two wolves,' Camilla carried on. She flicked through the book until she found the page she wanted, then held it up to show Ailsa. Two stylised wolves ran along over snowy ground. 'They were called Geri and Freki. Huginn and Muninn mean *thought* and *memory*, and Geri and Freki both mean *greedy*.'

'Both?'

Camilla shrugged. 'Apparently.'

'Do they test you on this stuff at the school where you live?'

'No,' Camilla said. 'I never really finish the work they give me. I spend all my time reading. I prefer it that way. Then I get to learn what I want to learn.'

'Don't you get into trouble?'

Camilla shrugged again. 'It doesn't really matter,' she said. 'When I leave school, I'm going to work for my dad's firm, anyway. I don't need to pass exams or anything for that.'

'Aye, I suppose,' Ailsa said.

She left Camilla to her gods and their pets. She imagined that two ravens followed her high above as she carried on to the clifftop paths. She imagined that Moxie had a twin, that they were both wolves running along beside her.

'Go away!' the strange woman spluttered. Her voice was quiet and hoarse. She sounded worn thin. The sadness in the cave washed over Ailsa. It threatened to engulf everything, it seemed.

'I brought you some things,' Ailsa said, shining her torch over the strange woman.

Moxie bounded over to her, sniffed her hair and curled up beside the rock pool.

'I don't want anything,' the woman hissed. 'Just . . . peace and quiet . . . Little *tosk*.'

'I got some more chocolate.'

The woman straightened a little where she lay. 'Oh,' she said. 'Well . . . aye, then . . .'

Ailsa sat down on a piece of rock and put her bag down before her. She was beginning to relax. The strange woman didn't scare her so much any more, especially not in the daytime. She unpacked some chocolate biscuits that she had pocketed at Uncle Nod and Aunt Bertha's. She unpacked a little bar of chocolate from a multipack.

'Come on . . . come on!' the strange woman hissed. She made a grab for it all, though her arms were weak. Her hands were feeble little claws, grasping at the air. Ailsa handed her a biscuit and waited as the strange woman curled her fingers around it.

'*Herlig . . . vakker . . .*' the strange woman sighed. She crammed the biscuit into her mouth and chomped away as Ailsa unpacked a little tin mug she had taken from the kitchen. She filled it from the rock pool and held it to the strange woman's lips.

The strange woman took a long draft. Some of the water dribbled down her chin. Then Ailsa helped her to eat another few biscuits.

'It's . . . it's wonderful what they do . . . with cocoa and sugar, these days,' the strange woman mumbled, still dribbling. 'The new things . . . they come up with . . . it's a surprise they're all such fools, coming out with this stuff.'

'Who's a fool?' Ailsa asked.

'All of them . . . of course.'

Ailsa thought about it. 'There's nothing new about chocolate biscuits,' she said.

'Depends how old you are,' the strange woman said.

'They've been around for ever, haven't they?'

'For ever's a long . . . long time, little one . . . I've seen enough of it to know . . .'

The strange woman gestured for some more water. Ailsa filled the tin cup and held it to her lips.

'Why do you sit in here all the time?' she asked as the strange woman drank. 'Don't you ever leave? Don't you want to?'

'Ha!' the strange woman barked a coarse laugh. It sounded like the crash of the surf on jagged rocks. 'There's nothing out there . . . for me, little one. Nothing but fools,' she said.

'Who are you? Really?'

'*Engelen . . . engelen av wann . . .*'

'What?'

'Angel . . . of the water . . .' the woman sighed. She leaned her head back and closed her eyes with a sad smile. 'Or I was . . . or something close . . . something like that . . .' she whispered. 'But who knows . . . any more? Who knows what I am . . . ?'

'I don't understand you,' Ailsa said.

''Cause you're a . . . fool, girl,' the strange woman said. 'One of the . . . one of the biggest ones going . . . I'd say.'

'I'm not.'

'Bah!'

'And you can't just sit here all day,' Ailsa said.

'Why not . . . ? There's nothing better to do . . . nowhere better to go.'

'There is,' Ailsa said. 'And there are lots of nice people too—'

'Bah! Go away!' the woman spat, opening her eyes. 'Fools . . . nothing out there . . . but fools . . .'

'Not everyone's a fool,' Ailsa said. 'My Aunt Bertha and Uncle Nod are really clever. They can mend any boat, no matter how old it is. No matter how broken it is.'

'Ha!' the woman croaked.

'And my mum's clever too, when . . . when she's well,' Ailsa said. 'And I know a girl. I just met her. She's really clever. Her name's Camilla and she knows all sorts of stories.'

'Fool stories!'

'Good stories, clever stories about ravens and wolves and old gods,' Ailsa insisted. 'If I brought her, you'd see how clever she was—'

'Pah! What could she know of the old gods?'

'—and her dad's Mr Galach and everyone says he's horrible, but he's also a really smart businessman too—'

'Galach?' the strange woman asked. A glint came to her eyes. They were wide open, all of a sudden, shining pale, icy blue out of the darkness. They looked like they burned cold.

'That's an old name from these parts . . .' she said. 'And I've known some of them . . . the Galachs . . . over the years . . .'

A strength seemed to bloom in her, though it was gone as fast as it came. Then she sagged and sat back, tired once more.

'Fine,' the strange woman whispered.

Moxie made a noise in the back of his throat.

'Fine?' Ailsa asked.

'Aye, fine,' the strange woman said. 'Bring the girl . . . with the clever father and her . . . fairy stories . . . of gods and monsters. Bring the Gallach girl . . . I will see for myself how smart she is . . .'

'Oh,' Ailsa said, not knowing quite what to say. She hadn't meant to suggest *actually* bringing Camilla. She had just been arguing a point.

'Now go away,' the strange woman snapped.

Ailsa realised that the sadness had lessened as they spoke, as she had fed the strange woman and sat with her. It rolled back, now, like a dense fog, chasing her as she left the cave.

Nine

Ailsa went to see Camilla the following morning. It was the hottest day so far that summer and all the grass was turning brown. The lane was cracked and dry, baked by the heady sunshine, and Aunt Bertha made Ailsa put extra sun cream on. Her skin was beginning to peel in long, white ribbons, but it no longer hurt too badly. It itched. It was annoying. But the deep pain in her joints was easing up, and it no longer felt like her skin was on fire.

The Galachs' gates were closed. Ailsa walked up to them tentatively. She craned her neck to see if Camilla was in the garden.

Camilla was sitting on a blanket in the shade of her tree. She had a notebook in front of her and loads of pencils scattered about. She looked up as Ailsa watched her. Ailsa blushed, caught staring, but Camilla smiled. She brushed her hair back behind her ears, pulled a little remote control out of her pocket and pressed a button. The gates began to slide open.

'Hello,' she said.

'Hi,' Ailsa replied. 'Can I come in?'

'Of course!' Camilla said. 'Come and sit with me.'

'Aye,' Ailsa said.

She went in. Moxie dashed in with her, wagging his tail. His tongue was lolling in the heat, and he was panting hard.

'Come into the shade, poor pooch!' Camilla said to Moxie, calling him over. She kneeled up and he bounded over to her, giving her a big lick. She giggled and he curled up gratefully by the great tree's trunk, out of the worst of the heat.

Camilla clicked the button again and the gates closed, sliding shut almost silently.

The Galachs' place was very large. The house was a grand stone building with a couple of smaller buildings clustered around it. The garden was a sweeping lawn dotted with trees and flower beds. It was dominated by a large pond, half empty in the heat. The pond was overlooked by a weeping willow. A path wound all the way around to the back of the house. Then, suddenly, it disappeared as it met the clifftops. The back of the house was almost right up against them. Beyond, the blue sea rolled away, flashing in the summer's sun.

'It's a sheer drop, right down,' Camilla said, seeing where Ailsa was looking. 'Cool, right?'

'Aye.'

'How's your mum doing?' Camilla asked.

Ailsa shrugged. 'She's still in bed and she won't move,' she said. 'She just lies there, in the dark, like she's half dead or something.'

'What exactly is wrong with her?'

Ailsa shrugged again. 'Her head, Aunt Bertha says. Uncle Nod says it's her heart. Maybe it's both. I don't know. It just happens sometimes. It's worse this time though, I think.'

Camilla was in the middle of drawing a picture. It was a tree with long branches and three lots of twisting roots going down deep into the earth.

'That's the one you told me about,' Ailsa said, nodding to it. 'The Viking tree.'

'Yggdrasil, yes,' Camilla said.

'You're good,' Ailsa said. 'At art, you know.'

Now Camilla blushed. She looked down at the picture. Then she looked back up at Ailsa and then down again.

'I've never been good at art,' Ailsa said. 'It never comes out right. Mum tried to teach me. She's really good at drawing and painting . . . you know, when she's not sick. She drew a picture of me as a baby and it looks really lifelike. It's in a frame by her bed back home.'

Camilla shaded a little bit of the tree. 'It just takes practice,' she said. 'And an eye for these things. Your mum must have a good eye.'

Camilla looked up. She smiled. 'What's wrong?' she asked. 'You look like you've got something on your mind.'

'Aye, well,' Ailsa said. 'I've got something I think I want to show you. Somewhere to take you.'

'Oh, that sounds exciting,' Camilla said. She jumped to her feet, ready to go, her drawing forgotten. 'What is it? Where is it?'

I met a strange woman in a cave and I don't know what to do . . .

She couldn't say the words, not now, but she felt

different this time. She felt at least like she could take Camilla, could include her in whatever madness was going on with her. The strange woman had asked her to bring Camilla along, after all, and that fact seemed to weigh heavily on Ailsa. It meant a lot to her. She had been thinking about it all night. Though she hadn't meant to involve Camilla with the strange woman at all – in fact, the thought had never occurred to her – she'd liked the sound of it by the time she had got up for breakfast. It was about time she shared it all with someone, and Camilla seemed like a good person for it.

'Not yet, not now,' Ailsa said.

'When, then?'

'Tonight,' Ailsa said. 'At like nine. It needs to be secret.'

'OK, wow,' Camilla said. 'I'll have to sneak out, though that's never been too much of a problem. My parents don't notice much. Where are we going . . . where should I meet you?'

'Meet me at the end of the road. I can't tell you where we're going, only show you.'

'A proper mystery!'

'Aye, well.'

Camilla started to gather up her art things a little while later, as the afternoon faded. 'I'll see you tonight, nine o'clock, at the end of the road,' she said.

'Aye.'

Camilla clicked the gates open for Ailsa then turned and hurried back off up to the house. Moxie stretched, yawned and came to Ailsa's side. He gave her hand a quick lick and then led the way home.

Mrs Tomlinson was in the kitchen with Aunt Bertha when she got back. They were both at the table, sipping tea from old, chipped mugs. Ailsa could hear Uncle Nod upstairs. It sounded as though he was singing in her mum's room, a sea shanty she had heard at the docks before.

'Such a softie,' Mrs Tomlinson said. She caught Ailsa's eye and winked. Then she raised an eyebrow as she saw Ailsa's sunburned skin.

'Oh my,' she said. 'You've been in the sun, then?'

'Aye,' Ailsa replied.

'It's been a couple of days,' Aunt Bertha said. She frowned.

Moxie stomped over to his bed in the corner of the kitchen and collapsed, exhausted from the heat.

'You need some aloe on it,' Mrs Tomlinson said.

'Oh, aye?' Aunt Bertha asked.

'Aye,' Mrs Tomlinson said. 'It takes the heat out of the skin. Moisturises it, too. Stops that peeling, there, and stops it from getting too sore.'

'Well, then.'

'They're sort of like wee cacti, aloe,' Mrs Tomlinson said. 'I grow them.'

Aunt Bertha nodded and sipped her tea.

'You're welcome to one,' Mrs Tomlinson carried on. 'I'll show you how to get the gel out and use it. Anything to help out, and all that.'

Mrs Tomlinson took Ailsa home with her. They went into her conservatory, a big glass structure at the back of her house. Pots of plants stood everywhere, overbursting. Ailsa saw her garden through the windows. The lawn was bare and brown from the heat, but the flowerbeds were vibrant. A coiled hose lay nearby, dribbling water.

One shelf in the conservatory held a row of ceramic pots with green, spikey plants growing in them. The plants were all thick, plumply jagged leaves standing up from the soil.

'This is them,' Mrs Tomlinson said, walking over to them with a pair of scissors. 'You cut a leaf, squeeze out the sap and rub it into your skin.'

She cut one of the leaves off and showed it to Ailsa. Using her thumb and forefinger, she squeezed the leaf like a tube of toothpaste. Pale green, translucent goo came out of the end she had cut.

'Try it, rub it into your skin,' she said.

Ailsa scooped some of the goo from Mrs Tomlinson's hand. It was cold and gloopy. She rubbed it between her palms and then onto her arms. There was instant relief from her sunburn. A cooling sensation washed over her skin.

'Oh, it's lovely,' she said. She was surprised, but Mrs Tomlinson smiled at her like she had expected nothing less.

'Aye,' Mrs Tomlinson said, picking up the pot and handing it to Ailsa. 'Now, you take this plant here. Put the aloe on a couple of times a day until your sunburn starts to go away. You'll be better in no time.'

'Aye, thank you, Mrs Tomlinson,' Ailsa said, taking the pot.

'Though be careful not to cut all the leaves,' Mrs Tomlinson said. 'We don't want it to die, now, do we? And water it, but only when the top couple of inches of the soil is dry. They don't get too thirsty, these ones.'

'Aye,' Ailsa said.

As she left, Ailsa turned to Mrs Tomlinson. 'Is it just for sunburn?'

'Sorry, love?' Mrs Tomlinson asked.

'The aloe,' Ailsa said. 'Is it just for sunburn, or can you use it for other things? For other kinds of . . . you know, hurt skin, like.'

'Aye, well, it's good for your skin in general,' Mrs Tomlinson said. 'Very moisturising, like I said. Eczema, rashes, sores . . . it's really quite wonderful stuff.'

'How do you use it for sores?' Ailsa asked.

'Oh dear, is your mum getting bedsores?' Mrs Tomlinson asked. 'I'd have thought your aunt and uncle would've—'

'No, I don't think so,' Ailsa said. 'They look after her, you know.'

'So, who's it for?'

'No one,' Ailsa said hurriedly. 'I'm just interested, you know. I'd never heard of aloe before.'

'Aye, well.' Mrs Tomlinson looked unconvinced, but she carried on. 'You clean sores. Soap or saltwater should do it. Then you put the aloe on, wrap them in bandages and let the aloe work its magic. Change the aloe and bandages often enough, keep the sores clean and dry, and they should heel up well. It's simple. I did it with my own mum when she was sick and took to her bed.'

She looked serious and frowned at Ailsa.

'Are you sure everything's OK, love?' she asked.

'Aye,' Ailsa said, backing out of the conservatory. 'Aye, it is. Thank you, Mrs Tomlinson!'

Moxie was waiting for her in the lane outside. He wagged his tail and gave a great, happy woof when he saw her.

'Come on, boy,' Ailsa said.

Ten

Ailsa met Camilla at the end of the road. Moxie jumped up and licked her face and she giggled breathlessly.

'I climbed out of my bedroom window,' Camilla whispered as they began to walk down to the coastal paths. 'How did you get out?'

Ailsa shrugged. 'Everyone's kind of busy, I guess,' she said. 'I just came out.'

'So, what's the big mystery?' Camilla asked.

'You'll see.'

'Sounds ominous.'

Ailsa shrugged again. 'I don't know what that means.'

'Worrying. Bad and scary.'

'Aye, then,' Ailsa said. 'Yeah, probably.'

'But it's safe?' Camilla asked, slightly alarmed.

'I guess so,' Ailsa replied. 'Safe enough, anyway. I've been down there a few times and I'm all right.' She paused for a few seconds. 'Would it matter if it wasn't safe?' she asked.

'No, of course not,' Camilla said. 'It's just, you know . . . it's good to be prepared for these kinds of things, isn't it?'

Ailsa held up a torch. She patted the rucksack she had slung over her shoulder. Inside the rucksack were a couple of aloe vera stalks she had cut along with some more chocolate and a few bits and pieces she thought might be useful.

'I'm prepared,' she said, though Camilla didn't look too reassured.

It didn't take them long to get to the beach with the cave. The sun was dipping down to the horizon, getting ready to set. Shadows danced on the rocks leading down from the cliffs. There was nevertheless enough light to see by.

'We can't get down there,' Camilla said. 'No one can, it's impassable. There's never been a path.'

'It's easy enough,' Ailsa said. 'Look, me and Moxie will show you.'

She was sure footed. Moxie ambled along beside her. Camilla marvelled. Where before it had always looked like there was no way down, suddenly a slim path opened up to them. It was lined with gorse bushes and hidden from above, but Ailsa guided them all down quite naturally.

'I was sure there wasn't a path there,' Camilla said. 'It's like it appeared from nowhere. Like it opened up just for us!'

Ailsa shrugged.

'Aye, I thought the same thing,' she said when they got to the bottom. 'Maybe it did. Who knows? Either way, it's easy, really.'

'So, is this the surprise?' Camilla asked. She was excited by it all. She gestured around the slim line of beach. 'A new beach, all to ourselves? How brilliant!'

'No, not really,' Ailsa said. She pointed at the cave. A few stones fell from the cliffs above, tinkling against the rockfaces. They pattered against the ground. 'The surprise is up in there.'

Camilla looked at her and frowned.

'Trust me,' Ailsa said.

Camilla nodded. Ailsa led her up the slim ridge of rock to the cave, feeling surprisingly brave. It felt good to be showing Camilla, to be bringing her in on the secret. It felt like Camilla was helping to share the burden.

As they walked along the slim ridge of rock, a few small pinpricks of light swirled through the water on either side. Ailsa felt as though she were being watched by something beneath the water.

'Be careful,' she whispered.

She switched on her torch when they stepped into the cave. Moxie ran ahead. Water dripped onto them from the ceiling above. Their footsteps echoed. Ailsa stepped out in front and lowered the torch's beam.

'*Tosk*!' the strange woman cursed.

Camilla screamed and let go of Ailsa's hand. She staggered backwards and stammered and began to breathe in shallow gasps.

'Don't worry,' Ailsa said. She was talking to both Camilla and the strange woman. The strange woman bared her sharp teeth and hissed, sitting up in the water.

Camilla turned and ran. She slipped as she got to the cave mouth, her feet going out from under her as she trod on a slimy patch of seaweed. She skidded, slid, went down onto her hands and knees and hit the cave wall.

'Camilla!' Ailsa cried out.

She ran over to Camilla, dropped down to her knees and put an arm around her. Camilla was breathing hard. She was shaking.

'What . . . what is that?' she asked, choking.

'It . . . *she* is why I brought you here,' Ailsa whispered. 'Come on, I want to introduce you.'

'I brought her, like you said, like I said,' Ailsa told the strange woman, pulling Camilla to her feet. 'She's Camilla, my friend, the girl I told you about.'

The strange woman bared her teeth again and glared at Camilla. There was fire in her eyes, Ailsa thought. But the strange woman nodded to herself after a few seconds. She closed her mouth and lowered her eyes.

Moxie whined and nuzzled the strange woman. The strange woman calmed down. She smiled to herself and patted him.

'*Glodhund* . . . sweet *glodhund*,' she crooned. 'All this fuss . . . sweet *glodhund*.'

'I brought you some things, too,' Ailsa said. She handed Camilla the torch.

Camilla took it with shaking hands. Her eyes were

wide and white as they met Ailsa's. Then Ailsa set her bag down at the side of the pool and crouched down. She took out the chocolate, some aloe and a roll of bandages.

'Bah!' the woman spat. She glared at the aloe and bandages. 'Sugar and cocoa and . . . nothing else . . . Everything else can go away!'

'I know a woman who says this stuff's good for sores,' Ailsa said. 'But she also said you're to keep dry . . .'

'Bah!'

The strange woman choked and spluttered. Ailsa picked up the tin mug she had left behind from last time and dipped it into the rock pool, filling it up.

'No,' Camilla whispered, quiet and hoarse. Her eyes were great circles and her cheeks were bright white. She was still shaking, but she looked at the mug and took a deep breath. 'Not saltwater,' Camilla said, her voice a little bolder. 'You can't drink saltwater. It will dehydrate you.' She gulped and the torch beam shook. 'It can send you mad.'

'Ha!' the strange woman cackled, wheezing, and Camilla stumbled back a little as though struck. 'Madness, madness . . . Saltwater is . . . in my blood, foolish little *dronning* . . . and it'll take more than you . . . to change my ways . . .'

The strange woman panted. She was tired. Her voice was a raw whisper. Ailsa held the mug up to her lips and the strange woman let some of the water slip down her throat. She sighed and nodded.

'I'll leave you the chocolates if you let me treat your sores,' Ailsa said.

'It'll take more than that . . . to fix me . . .' the woman said. Her eyes glinted, though she smiled lightly. The expression was odd, more of a grimace, and her sharp teeth glimmered in the torchlight. 'Raw skin doesn't heal . . . if it's incomplete . . .'

'What do you mean?'

'Nothing . . . nothing, little one,' the strange woman said. She glared at Ailsa, but she nodded. It was a small, brief gesture. 'Bandages, then . . . but you'll not keep me . . . dry . . . I shouldn't think.'

'W-what . . . I mean, *who* are you?' Camilla stammered.

Ailsa looked around at her as the strange woman cackled once more. Camilla's face was pale, and her lip trembled, but her eyes were alight.

She is as excited as she is nervous, Ailsa realised.

'Ha!' the strange woman cackled. '*What* am I . . . ha! What, what . . . what . . .' It seemed like she wouldn't answer for a long moment. She regarded Camilla with a cold gaze. 'An old fool . . . a relic and worse,' she said. 'That's what I am . . . it's *who* I am, too, I'd reckon . . . little *dronning*.'

'You're d-dying,' Camilla said.

'Ha! Aren't we all? Dying, dying. Always dying . . . never dead . . . until we are.'

'Y-you . . . you can't stay here.'

'Away with you, little *dronning*.'

'What does that mean, "*dronning*"?' Ailsa asked.

'Queen . . . Little queen . . . little queen of the land. I told you I knew her family . . . all little princelings, building their castles . . .'

'You know my family?' Camilla asked. A look of astonishment plastered itself across her face.

'*Knew*, girl, *knew*,' the strange woman croaked. 'Once upon a time . . . a long, long time ago . . .' She choked.

Ailsa filled up the cup once more and fed her some more water. Then Ailsa picked up the aloe and bandages.

'I've told her she needs to come out, to get proper help,' Ailsa told Camilla.

The strange woman snorted.

'But she won't let me do anything.'

'Have you told anyone?' Camilla asked.

'Only you. I couldn't tell anyone else. I wanted to, but I couldn't. I don't know why.' Ailsa turned back to the strange woman. 'We need you out of there while we put these on,' she said.

The strange woman shrugged. She allowed them to pull her out of the rock pool but offered no help. Ailsa and Camilla each took an arm, though Camilla looked like she didn't want to go anywhere near the woman. Her skin was cold and clammy. It felt slightly scaled beneath Ailsa's fingers. She was careful to avoid the sores and weals that shaped themselves over the strange woman's shoulders and chest.

They both braced to heave, but the woman came out easily enough. She was painfully thin and light as air, nearly. The water barely rippled as she came out and, as they sat her against the back of the cave, they saw how small she was. She was shorter than either of them, and shrunken, like she was folding in on her own bones. Her ribs poked out and her hip bones and shoulders looked sharp.

Her skin was pale and bare, but she didn't shiver. Long nails like talons curled from her fingers. Slivers of seaweed and patches of silt clung to her. Her sores carried on down her chest and grew worse as they laced over her hips and legs. Her shins and calves were red raw and inflamed. They looked like they were missing a layer of skin. Her feet were gnarled, bloody and malformed, twisted towards one another.

Camilla wrinkled her nose. Ailsa didn't, though she had to fight the urge to choke. Out of the water, the stench of rotten fish and worse rose from the strange woman.

'But your eyes,' Camilla whispered. Her fear seemed forgotten as she gazed at the strange woman.

'Aye,' Ailsa said.

The strange woman's eyes were indeed beautiful up close, in the torch's light. Blue, grey and green played through one another, swirling around large pupils. Silver glittered around their edges, cold and lively. They seemed ever so deep, too. They seemed to go forever inwards, and they were sad. The sadness Ailsa always felt in the cave radiated from them.

'Well,' the strange woman said. She closed her eyes and set her head back against the cave wall. 'I wasn't always a relic . . . I wasn't always broken . . .'

'Who are you?' Camilla asked.

'Nobody . . .' the strange woman said. 'Not any more. And not yet.'

'How do you know . . . how *did* you know my family?' Camilla carried on.

Ailsa was surprised at the look on Camilla's face. She was surprised to see Camilla so stunned, so concerned.

'Through the deep sea and the high waves . . .' the strange woman told her. 'We're all salt soaked . . . all sea dogs, after all . . .'

'Riddles,' Camilla said.

'Aye . . . but they'll have to do . . . for the moment,' the strange woman said, faltering.

She let them work on her. Ailsa squeezed the sap from an aloe leaf like Mrs Tomlinson had shown her. She rubbed it between her palms. Camilla took some and between them they carefully rubbed it over the strange woman's skin, over her chest and hips, into her legs. The strange woman hissed in pain, and they pulled back from her calves. 'No . . . go on,' she said. 'It is cooling . . . it helps.'

Sure enough, within a little while of rubbing it in, the strange woman sighed in satisfaction.

'It carries the deep cold of the earth and water,' she said. 'Like the surf . . . and the rocks beneath . . .'

Moxie gave her a sniff, nuzzling at the drying aloe, and he wagged his tail. Ailsa and Camilla cut lengths of bandages and wrapped them around her upper arms and chest.

'We'll not be able to do your legs if you're going back into the water,' Ailsa told the strange woman. 'That'll just make things worse.'

'Are you sure you won't stay out of the water?' Camilla asked. 'Give everything a chance to heal properly.'

'Aye, your sores can get better, I think,' Ailsa said. 'But not here. It's too damp. And definitely not underwater.'

The woman laughed. Her laughter was softer now. It had lost its coarse edge. It had lost some of its malice.

'And besides,' Camilla ventured. She picked up a large rock that looked like it had fallen from the ceiling not too long ago. 'These cliffs are old and crumbling.'

'Aren't we all . . . ?'

'They're crumbling *quickly*,' Camilla said. 'There are signs everywhere. Daddy has had people out to the house, looking at the cliffs, at the foundations . . . the whole area is subsiding, falling into the sea. Just last year, a load of cliffs collapsed and caught a couple of kids in them. They could have been killed. As it was, it took hours to dig them out. The same thing could happen to you if you stay here, and you might not survive. Probably won't, in fact.'

'There's nowhere else . . .' the strange woman said. 'You tell your daddy . . . nowhere else for some of us. Just a crumbling cave and a . . . and a slow burial . . .'

'But that's just it,' Camilla said. She clapped her hands together. Her eyes shone as her whole face lit up. Ailsa thought it looked as though she was about to burst with an idea.

'I think there may be somewhere else,' Camilla carried on, 'while your skin heals and you get your strength back.'

'Get my strength back . . .' the woman whispered. She opened her eyes, her beautiful, sad eyes and looked up at Camilla. 'Little *dronning*, get my strength back . . . indeed . . .'

'I'll sort it all out,' Camilla said. She looked at Ailsa, all fear forgotten. '*We* will sort it out,' she said.

Moxie's throat rumbled happily, and he wagged his tail some more.

'Just leave the sugar and cocoa, little one,' the strange woman told Ailsa. 'Forget the rest.'

'No,' Ailsa said. 'No, we can help you.'

They left the chocolate and a full mug of water. They lowered the strange woman back into her pool and she sighed with relief as she settled into it.

Camilla looked back as they left.

'What's your name?' she asked.

The strange woman's voice came to them through the growing darkness.

'Go away,' she said.

They climbed back up the cliffside in silence. They held hands as they walked back home along the twisting clifftop path. Camilla was white and ashen from the shock, but she seemed quite calm, now.

'Is it true?' Ailsa asked. 'About the cliffs, and that? That they're crumbling that fast?'

'Yes,' Camilla said.

'We have to find her somewhere else, then.'

Camilla nodded. 'I think I have a plan,' she said as they turned onto their road. 'Let me think it through a bit, though. Come round to mine tomorrow at about two. We'll be able to sort it out then.'

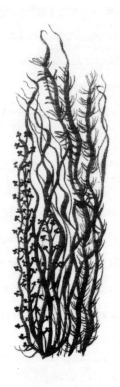

Eleven

Ailsa went to Camilla's house the following day. Camilla was waiting for her by the gate. She led Ailsa through the garden, up some steps to the side of the house and in through a side door.

'We don't use the main doors very much,' she said. 'They're too big. We only open them for special parties and things.'

The side door opened into a wide, airy entrance hall. A flight of stairs climbed up one end. There was a locked door to one side.

'My dad's office,' Camilla said. 'It's right at the back. The windows overlook the cliffs and the sea. It's a really beautiful view, though he never lets us go in there.'

She smiled mischievously at Ailsa. 'I can still get in whenever I want, though,' she said. 'He doesn't know I can, but it's easy enough.'

There were pictures on the walls, photos of family members. One man cropped up a few times in them, first as a young man, then finally in his old age. He had flinty eyes. He was smiling in all of the pictures, though Ailsa thought he never managed to look very happy.

'That's my grandfather,' Camilla said, seeing Ailsa looking. 'Grandpa Peter.'

'The one who was into all the myths?' Ailsa asked.

Camilla nodded. 'He started the family business and built this house,' she said. 'He died when I was only little. A boating accident.'

There was a large, open living room off the hall. A younger girl was sitting at a table in the window, painting pictures of fish with watercolours. A woman was sitting on a white leather sofa, looking at a magazine. Ailsa noticed that her eyes weren't moving. Her jaw was tight. A man was pacing around a smaller, adjoining room, whispering fiercely into a phone.

'Hello, darling,' the woman said as Camilla led Ailsa

in. She didn't put the magazine down, nor did she stop looking at it.

'This is Ailsa,' Camilla said.

The little girl at the table stopped painting and looked up, glaring at Ailsa.

'She's Nod and Bertha's niece,' Camilla told them.

'Nod and . . . ?' her mum began.

'From up the road,' Camilla said. 'They fix up all the boats.'

'Oh, yes, of course,' her mum said.

'Ailsa, this is my mum. And this is Suzanne, my sister,' Camilla said, gesturing to the small girl at the table. 'That's Dad, in the other room.'

'Aye, hello,' Ailsa mumbled.

Mr Galach ended his phone call and came through from the other room. She recognised him from some of the photos in the hallway. His eyes looked hard, and his skin was flushed. Ailsa was surprised by how tall and skinny he was. He seemed to loom over the whole room.

He's a real gangster, Ailsa thought, remembering what the fishermen had said of him, what Uncle Nod had said of him. Mean and brutal. She could see it in his eyes, in his face, in every line of his body. He looked like a beast, ready to hunt, ready to hurt.

'This is Ailsa,' Camilla told him.

Mr Galach looked at Ailsa. His face didn't move but his eyes flashed like they were laughing at his own private joke.

'I've seen you running about with that great big German Shepherd,' he said.

'Moxie?' Ailsa asked. 'Aye. But I think he's a Belgian Shepherd cross.'

Mr Galach shrugged. 'Some form of Shepherd,' he said. He turned to Camilla's mum. 'I'm going out. Things to see to.'

Mrs Galach didn't answer. Mr Galach strode from the room, crossing it in a few strides and then crashing out through the door. Mrs Galach put her magazine down when he was gone.

'Come on,' Camilla said, tugging at Ailsa's hand. 'We'll go up to my room.'

They sat in her room for a few minutes without saying too much. Ailsa watched the sunlight darting in through the window. Camilla toyed with a discarded book on her bed. Then she laughed, then she frowned.

'We need to help her,' she said.

Ailsa nodded. She thought of the strange woman and the desire to fix her, to help her, welled up inside her.

'Aye,' she said. 'She can't stay down in that cave. She's dying, I think. She'll die if she stays down there. I just know it.'

'I think so too,' Camilla agreed. 'It's not safe down there, anyway. And she's so unhappy. I could feel it, deep down in my bones.'

'I know,' Ailsa said. 'It's like it's stuck to the rocks, like it's in the air. It's horrible.'

'Yes, well, I've been thinking about it,' Camilla said. 'There is somewhere we can take her.'

'Aye?'

'Daddy's lighthouse.'

'Oh. Aye. Aye,' Ailsa said, brightening.

'It's deserted,' Camilla said. 'Nobody's allowed to go in. The architect isn't due to look at it for another few months.'

'It's perfect,' Ailsa said. She leaned forwards, excited. She could imagine it. It would be brilliant.

'We can leave her with some food and bits while she gets her strength back.'

111

'And we can visit her whenever we want, to check she's OK,' Ailsa concurred. 'When can we move her?'

'Tonight. I can slip out and meet you at midnight.'

'Aye,' Ailsa said. 'Aye.'

Ailsa checked the alarm clock. It was half past eleven, time to get up. She had been dreaming of drowning once more. First her mum drowned, then she drowned, then her mum turned into her, and she watched herself drown. Her sheets were damp with sweat as she kicked them aside.

She dressed warmly for the night and then tiptoed through into her mum's room. Moxie stirred. He padded along behind her, yawning his head off.

Her mum was as pale as ever as the moonlight filtered in through the window. Her face was serene, and her chest barely moved as she lay there.

'My sweetheart,' her mum mumbled in her sleep as Ailsa took her hand.

'It's OK, Mum,' Ailsa replied. 'You get your rest.'

Ailsa left her mum, went outside and took a wheelbarrow from the yard on her way to the meeting point. Moxie followed her silently.

Camilla was already waiting for her. The moon and stars shone brightly overhead, and she was haloed in silver. She looked terrified, her eyes wide and white, like Ailsa had been the first couple of times she had gone to visit the strange woman.

Like she felt now, too, if she was honest with herself. She still wasn't comfortable sneaking out along the cliffs at night, going down to that awful cave.

'I wasn't sure that you were really coming,' Camilla said.

'Why wouldn't I come?' Ailsa asked.

'I wasn't sure that I was coming, to be honest.'

'But you did.'

'Yes.'

'And you want to carry on?'

'Yes.'

'Aye, well then,' Ailsa said.

Moxie padded out of the dark behind her, the silvery light catching on his fur. Camilla kneeled to hug him and scratch him behind the ears. He wagged, thumping his great tail from side to side.

'He's like your shadow,' Camilla said.

Ailsa shrugged. 'Sometimes I feel more like his,' she said.

'His shadow?'

'Aye.'

'Don't be daft,' Camilla said.

Ailsa shrugged again. 'We'd best get going,' she said.

They had each brought a torch, though they didn't really need to use them. For the most part, the moon and stars were bright enough to light their way. Even the sea shone with it all, catching, breaking and scattering the light as each wave came in.

'That's got to be a good sign,' Camilla said, her voice quaking a little. 'It's like nature wants us to do this.'

'Aye, well, maybe.'

It sounded more like Camilla was trying to reassure herself. Ailsa was still unsure. She was unsure about all of it, and her heart had begun to race again, beating hard. Her hands were shaking slightly, and she found herself jumping at every little noise and shadow. They had felt so sure when they planned all this. But now, in the darkness of night, nothing felt certain. Nothing felt safe.

They left the wheelbarrow on the cliffs as they went down to the cove. They climbed down to the beach guided by the moon and star light, wending along the hidden, twisting path. The lighthouse winked away along the coastal path. Its automated light cut through the night and the moon and all.

'It looks so far away from here,' Camilla said.

'It's not so bad,' Ailsa replied, though she secretly agreed. It all seemed so much. She took a deep breath though, and squared her shoulders.

The slab of rock leading up to the cave mouth rose a few feet from the water. The sea was calm as it lapped at the beach. Everything else was quiet and still. They climbed up to the cave. Moxie led them, Camilla tiptoed after him, and Ailsa came up last.

'I'm scared,' Camilla whispered as they were about to go in. Her voice shook. 'Aren't you scared?'

'Aye, I am,' Ailsa replied. 'But then I think about the sadness. You know? Nobody should be that sad.'

'Yes.' Camilla sighed and straightened up. 'You're right,' she said. 'Come on then.'

They went inside, using their torches in earnest for the first time that night.

'Look, already,' Camilla whispered, pointing her torch

down at the floor just inside the cave's mouth. Some stalactites had fallen from the ceiling, shattering against the floor. The wall next to them shivered with dust, a great split scouring upwards.

'Burying me alive, or worse,' the strange woman said from the back of the cave. Her voice was hoarse. It crept through the darkness in a scratching sigh and Camilla jumped, breathing quickly.

Ailsa shone her torch forwards, finding the strange woman's face. She squinted and turned aside, hissing.

'Point that . . . somewhere else, *tosk*,' she cursed.

'Oh, sorry, aye,' Ailsa said. She pointed the beam at the ground and came over to the rock pool. The strange woman was where she always was, half slumped in the water, her head lolling weakly on her neck.

'You're back then, little one,' the strange woman said, glaring up at Ailsa. 'And you, too . . . little *dronning*,' she said to Camilla.

Her hair hung lank and knotted about her shoulders and her eyes glimmered. Moxie bounded over to her side and gave her face a gentle lick. Camilla shook, still scared, still uncomfortable in the strange woman's presence.

116

'Ah . . . foolish *glodhund*,' the strange woman sighed. She took Moxie's face in one frail hand, closed her eyes and touched her forehead to his.

'We-we've come to rescue you,' Camilla stuttered breathlessly.

'Ha!' the strange woman laughed.

'Aye, but really,' Ailsa said. 'We have.'

'Yes, you can't stay here,' Camilla said. Her voice grew a little bolder. 'It's not safe. And it's nowhere for anyone to live. You can't be happy or healthy here. We've got somewhere you can stay for a bit.'

'Aye,' Ailsa chimed in. 'Somewhere you can get your strength back.'

'Why can't you just . . . leave me be?' the strange woman asked. She sank slightly deeper into her rock pool.

Ailsa walked around the water. Some of the stone came away under her weight. It crumbled into small pieces and fell into the rock pool. Camilla went the other way, to the strange woman's other side. She had to push past Moxie, who seemed thoroughly excited by it all.

'I . . . I can't,' the strange woman said. She choked. It sounded half like a sob.

'Why not?' Camilla asked.

'She's scared,' Ailsa said. 'Aren't you?'

She kneeled down by the strange woman and placed a hand on her shoulder. The skin was as cold and clammy as ever.

'Aye, little one,' the strange woman whispered. 'It's been so long . . . since I left this place . . . I was happy . . . no, I wasn't, but I had made my peace, I had given up, I was ready for the end, for death . . . until you came . . .'

Camilla bent down to the strange woman, any fear she might have been feeling herself seemingly forgotten. She placed her own forehead against the strange woman's hair. Moxie snuggled in. Ailsa stayed where she was, holding the strange woman's shoulder.

'It's safe, where we're taking you,' Ailsa said. She spoke in a very quiet voice and the strange woman nodded.

The strange woman tried to rise and failed. Her limbs didn't have the strength. She half-sobbed again and Ailsa and Camilla caught hold of her. They lifted her up. She was as light as ever. Her bare, cold skin was blue and her raw, crooked feet made Ailsa shudder as they broke out of the water.

'Come on,' Ailsa said. 'I've got some bits for you.'

They leaned the strange woman against the cave wall and Ailsa opened her rucksack. She pulled out a towel and handed it to Camilla, who began to pat the strange woman dry. Then she and Camilla unwound the strange woman's bandages. They were wet through. The skin was pink and new beneath, however, refreshed across her shoulders, ribs and hips. They rubbed some more aloe into it. They rubbed some into the strange woman's legs and ankles, though they left her feet, and wound clean bandages around it all. Finally, Ailsa pulled an old jumper and a pair of jogging bottoms from her bag, and they dressed the strange woman.

They had to roll the trousers and the sleeves of the jumper up several times to fit the strange woman. The jumper's hem came halfway down her thighs like a smock.

'You'll be nice and warm, now.'

'Bah,' the strange woman said half-heartedly.

They had the strange woman out of the cave, up the winding path and onto the clifftops a short while later. She was so light that she was easy enough to carry and move, though she groaned in pain every so often. Her breathing grew hoarse and ragged.

They put her in the wheelbarrow, wrapped her in a blanket, and Ailsa began to trundle her onwards. Camilla went ahead to lead them. Huffing, panting, they made their way around the coast towards the lighthouse. Their journey took them through winding tracks, slim paths and steep, scree laden slopes. Ailsa saw a couple of foxes. She even thought she saw a doe at one point.

'Landlubbers . . . but beautiful enough,' the strange woman sighed, staring after them. 'Beautiful . . . beautiful . . .' Her voice jangled as the wheelbarrow bumped along. All around, the sounds of a quiet night and the wash of the sea so far below whispered to them.

They arrived at the lighthouse, tired and breathing hard from taking turns pushing the wheelbarrow. A level path led along the finger of rock to the lighthouse itself and the wheelbarrow became a lot smoother as they got close to it, suddenly seeming to glide along.

They passed the small outhouses, each one outlined in the shimmering moonlight. There was a short set of steps leading up to the lighthouse's front door. Camilla helped

Ailsa up with the wheelbarrow. Then she went to the door itself, pulling a set of keys from her pocket. She fumbled with them until she found the right one.

The lock creaked as she slid the key in and turned it. The hinges squealed with rust as she pushed the door open. Ailsa waited, unsure, as the darkness within the lighthouse seemed to loom. However, Camilla's voice floated out brightly a few seconds later.

'All good,' she called back to them.

Ailsa took up the wheelbarrow once more and bumped it over the threshold. The strange woman mumbled and groaned as she was tossed about.

'Oh, sorry!' Ailsa said as they got across the threshold. She put the wheelbarrow down and took a hold of the strange woman. Camilla rushed to the other side, and they each draped one of the strange woman's arms around their shoulders, lifting her light body clear of the wheelbarrow.

Everywhere inside was dark and dusty. A wide main hallway opened up. A slim passageway led away from it. Ailsa could see a kitchen and bathroom at its end. Stairs ran up from opposite the front door.

'They go into the main house bit,' Camilla told her. 'Then there's another staircase up into the tower. Daddy took me up there when I first got back from school.'

They went upstairs, carrying the strange woman between them, as Moxie ran about the whole house, sniffing away. A door opposite the top of the stairs opened into a large living space. Threadbare carpets lay all about. There was a small balcony behind a tall set of closed French doors.

The strange woman's breathing looked shallow as they laid her on the ground, still draped in her oversize jumper and trousers. Ailsa thought she had never looked smaller.

'Here,' Ailsa said, rummaging in her rucksack once more. She pulled out a cushion and a blanket and laid them down to make the strange woman as comfortable as possible. Then she set half a packet of chocolate biscuits down next to her.

Camilla set a spare key down.

'It's your home now,' she told the strange woman.

'And we'll come back tomorrow with more food,' Ailsa said, but the strange woman had already closed her eyes.

It looked to Ailsa as though she had fallen into an uneasy sleep, her breath shallow and her skin pallid and wan.

They left her, locked the door behind themselves and walked back along the finger, taking turns once more to push the wheelbarrow. The first light of dawn was touching the horizon. This far north, the dawn always came early in the summertime. Far off, they could see the first few fishing boats leaving the harbour.

'I'll see you tomorrow . . . or, later today,' Camilla said as they got to her house.

'Aye,' Ailsa replied, yawning. She felt completely shattered.

Twelve

Ailsa managed a few hours of sleep before Uncle Nod came to knock on her door.

'Come on, love, you'll snooze the day away,' he said.

'Aye, Uncle Nod,' she replied groggily.

'I'll get you some breakfast going, love.'

'Aye, thank you.'

She sat at the kitchen table sipping tea and staring at the wall. It seemed to shift and spin, she was so tired from the night before.

'You not sleeping properly, love?' Uncle Nod asked.

'Not really.'

'Aye, well. Perhaps we could speak to Dr Arbuthnot about it next time he's here.'

'No,' Ailsa said. 'No, it's just . . . bad dreams. They'll go, I'm sure.'

'We'll see,' Uncle Nod said.

She munched her cereal, enjoying the sugar as it hit her and perked her up a little. Uncle Nod watched her.

'Come on,' he said when she was done. 'I'm to go out onto the water today to check on some bits and pieces in the docks. Why don't you come with me?'

'Aye,' Ailsa said. She always loved going out on the water with him. 'Yes please.'

The docks were empty. Half the boats were out on the water. The other half were left moored, unattended and slightly dilapidated. Moxie trotted alongside Ailsa as she followed Uncle Nod. He jumped into Uncle Nod's little skiff and settled in as she climbed down into it.

Uncle Nod rowed them from point to point around the harbour. Warm sunlight skimmed the water. It broke against the wake left by Uncle Nod's oars.

'Did you ever hear the story of King Canute?' Uncle Nod asked as he rowed.

'No.'

'Aye, well,' Uncle Nod began. 'King Canute was a great ancient king who ruled a thousand years ago. He was a king in England, in Norway and in Denmark.'

125

'All of them?'

'Aye,' Uncle Nod said. 'He was a big deal, I guess. But he wasn't always comfortable with it, by most accounts. The story is that he went down to the coast one day and tried to hold back the tide, which, of course, he couldn't do.

'People get it wrong, though,' Uncle Nod explained. 'They think it's a story about a mad king who thought he was able to hold back the power of nature itself. But that's a load of rubbish. It's not the original story, it's not its meaning.'

They passed by a very old fishing boat. Barnacles clung to its side, the wood was warped in places and a couple of old nets hung over the side, covered in clinging seaweed. Uncle Nod tutted and shook his head when he saw the state it was in.

'What is the meaning?' Ailsa asked.

'Well, King Canute was indeed a very powerful king,' Uncle Nod said. 'So he had plenty of brown-nosers sucking up to him and what not. Telling him he was the best, just so they could win his favour. Well, he wanted none of it. He was just a man, after all. And he wanted to show his followers and courtiers that he was just a man. So, he tried to hold back the tide, knowing full well that he would fail.'

'Why would he do that?'

'So that they could see he didn't have limitless power, that he was no god,' Uncle Nod said. 'Only God could hold back the tides, he said. The fact that he couldn't showed everyone how powerless he truly was.'

They went out to a couple more fishing boats, tied at the far end. Uncle Nod checked their hulls. He checked their motors. He climbed aboard one and had a poke around on the deck as Ailsa watched. He shook his head some more and kept tutting.

'Some folks,' he complained as he climbed back down into the skiff. 'They just don't know how to take care of things. They ask me to come out and see to their boats, but if they were just a bit more careful themselves, there'd be half the issues cropping up. I've my work cut out with this lot.'

'Isn't that a good thing?' Ailsa asked. 'It means you've got lots of customers.'

'Aye,' Uncle Nod conceded. 'Though half of them won't be able to pay half of what's owed. It's the way of things.

And it's the principle involved. I like to see folks taking good care of what's important, you know?'

'Aye.'

Moxie's ears pricked up as they rowed back across the harbour towards the docks. He began to whine, and his hackles rose as he reared up from the bottom of the boat. Nose twitching, he began to sniff at the water. Something down there moved, swooping through the water a few feet down.

'Ach, away with you, you daft beggar,' Uncle Nod said. 'It'll just be a couple of wee fishes or a seal or something. Likely nothing. Stop getting so het up, pal.'

But Moxie wouldn't be dissuaded. Uncle Nod sighed and shook his head and continued to row them back.

Ailsa leaned over to see what Moxie was getting so excited about. The water churned as the oars cut through it. Then Moxie's whining rose, getting louder. Something broke the surface about a hundred yards or so away.

'See, just a seal,' Uncle Nod grunted. 'You see them sometimes. Foolish mutt.'

He is right, Ailsa thought. A seal's head was sticking out of the water, gazing towards them. She had seen one before, when she was staying at Aunt Bertha and Uncle Nod's a couple of summers ago. It looked like a large, wet spaniel. Moxie wagged his tail hard. Ailsa had to hold onto him to stop him from jumping into the water. She pulled him to the middle of the boat, everything rocking as she did so. The seal was gone the next time she looked up.

'Stupid animal!' Uncle Nod cursed.

Something moved under the water. It glinted in the sunlight.

'What's that?' Ailsa asked. She pointed down. As she did so, a couple of lights flickered on and off down there.

'What now?' Uncle Nod sighed.

The lights flickered again. They seemed to follow the boat. Then a couple more lights flickered, circling.

They're not flickering, Ailsa thought.

They're blinking, watching.

'What is it?' Uncle Nod asked.

'A pair of . . . I don't know,' Ailsa said. As she watched, she caught another flicker. Then the lights were gone, swiftly swallowed by the water. Whatever had been watching them dived out of sight.

'You two, honestly,' Uncle Nod said, shaking his head. 'Like two peas in a pod, both as daft as each other.'

'Aye, maybe,' Ailsa said. She still felt as though she were being watched.

Moxie stood motionless on the jetty when they got out. He was alert, his front paw raised like he was hunting, staring out over the water as Uncle Nod tied the boat up.

'Come on, you wee fool,' Uncle Nod called back as he threw a coil of rope over his shoulder and began to walk away. 'You too, Ailsa. There's work that needs doing.'

Ailsa nodded and made to follow, though she was reluctant to turn her back on the water. It wasn't her imagination. She was sure of it. Something out there was watching.

Thirteen

They went back to the lighthouse that night when everyone else was asleep. Moxie ran ahead, straight up the stairs. His head was high, his whole body excited, far more so than usual. Ailsa and Camilla followed closely behind. Ailsa secretly wondered what they would find within. There was still so much about the strange woman that they didn't know.

The lights were all off inside. The smell of brine lay faintly over everything. The windows were all dusty and grimy, salt-stained from the sea, so that a dirty patina of faint moonlight struggled in. All else was darkness, layered with shadows, hidden by them.

It was beginning to feel like the cave.

The briny smell grew stronger with each step. It seemed

131

to creep through the place like a fog, stinging Ailsa's nose, making her gag slightly. As they headed upstairs, it grew potent enough that she fancied she could indeed almost see it lingering in the air. It was coming from inside the strange woman's room, they realised as they approached it.

The door was slightly ajar from where Moxie had clearly nudged his way in. Ailsa pushed it fully open. It was damp and cold. Her fingers came away with a faint coating of grime upon them. Camilla followed, breathing carefully, trying not to touch anything.

The balcony doors inside were thrown wide. The briny smell layered around the room and the salt spray from outside joined with it. It was at once fresh and putrid. It was rot and it was new life.

Ailsa and Camilla found the strange woman slumped on the balcony's floor, resting against the doorframe. She had her legs crossed and her eyes closed, and she was facing out to sea as the strong, salty breeze whipped in at her. Her hair was flying all around her face and she breathed deeply, looking almost happy for the first time. The clothes and blanket Ailsa had given her were thrown to one side, abandoned as the strange woman felt the wind against her bare skin. Moxie was curled up beside her.

It took Ailsa a few seconds to realise that the strange woman was singing. There were no words, but her mouth was open, and her lungs were working raggedly beneath her ribs. What came out was quiet and sorrowful. It was primal, beautiful. It seemed to mix with the crash of waves far below and the violent winds coming in from the open sea. It harmonised with them. It fit them perfectly.

Then the strange woman stopped. The wind died down and the song was finished. The air freshened slightly, letting the girls breathe a little more easily. However, something was lost. The power, almost overwhelming, died away. A great sadness replaced it, sadness and decay.

The strange woman turned to face Ailsa and Camilla, smiled and then sagged to the balcony's floor, exhausted.

They both rushed over to her. They half carried her back inside and settled her on the blanket, but she just laughed, faint and wheezy. She cackled, then she coughed and choked where she lay.

It was all too much for Ailsa. The cave itself, the transformation in the lighthouse, the strange woman and her incredibly strange ways. She had gone along with her in ignorance for long enough.

Now she wanted answers.

The strange woman looked up at her with a glint in her eye, half challenging, like she knew what Ailsa was thinking.

'Oh, aye then,' she whispered. 'Tell me . . . what questions have you got for me . . . little one?'

Ailsa took a deep breath. There was no going back from this point. She was a little scared by the thought of what the strange woman might tell her. She was even more scared by the thought that the strange woman might not tell her anything at all.

But the moment had come. There was nothing else for it.

'What are you?' Ailsa asked.

The woman shrugged one bony shoulder and fixed Ailsa with her gaze. Her eyes were fierce and unwavering, as beautiful as ever.

'You have to tell us,' Camilla said.

She was desperate to know, Ailsa thought. She looked like it was the most urgent thing in the world as she leaned forwards, towards the strange woman.

'Foolish little *dronning*,' the strange woman snapped. Her voice was hoarse and brutal, nothing like it had been when she was singing. 'I know that already. Look, look at this one . . .' she gestured at Ailsa. 'She has steel in her nerves . . . in her eyes . . . The little one will have her answers . . . no?'

Ailsa nodded. 'It's time,' she said.

'Aye . . . aye . . . maybe . . .' the strange woman said. 'Though what can a child know of waiting . . . ?'

Her chest shook and her breathing was light and shallow. For a long moment, Ailsa wondered if she was going to answer at all.

'I am many and I am one . . . And I am me . . . most of all . . .' the strange woman eventually said very quietly.

'What does that mean?' Ailsa asked. She was getting sick of the strange woman's nonsense. It was impossible to get a straight answer out of her.

'Ha!' the strange woman laughed once more, choking a little this time. 'I don't know myself, not any more . . . I'm trying to remember it, and these . . . these funny little riddles . . . are all I've had for such a long time . . . all that I have been, I suppose . . .'

135

She took a deep, shuddering breath, closed her eyes, opened them, and looked at Ailsa.

'Silly men have . . . named me more times than I can count . . .' she said, then her voice faded. 'Foolish names . . . names that spoke of everything and nothing, ancient names that could hardly count next to the many years I have seen . . . But some names . . . some have lasted. Selkie, they called me, in these parts . . .'

'Your name is Selkie?' Camilla asked.

'Foolish *dronning*,' the strange woman snapped. 'They called me *a* selkie, in their stupidity . . . Others have called me by many different names . . . mermaiden . . . siren . . . spirit, nymph . . . all men's folly, of course.'

'Like a real mermaid?' Camilla asked. 'Like real spirits?'

The strange woman shook her head. 'What is real, anyway . . . ?' she asked. 'I am certainly flesh and . . . blood. Or something like it. So yes . . . real enough, too real, maybe . . .'

'But what's your name?' Ailsa demanded. 'What do you call yourself?'

For a long moment, she thought once again that the

strange woman wouldn't answer. The strange woman just lay in their arms, her eyes closed, catching her breath.

Finally, she spoke.

'Hefring,' she said. 'That's the first name I remember them calling me. It is the name my mother gave me.'

'Hefring,' Ailsa repeated.

The strange woman nodded.

'I . . . I think I know that name,' Camilla said.

The strange woman, Hefring, nodded again. 'I wondered if you might, little *dronning*.'

'From the old stories, the Norse myths,' Camilla continued. 'In one of my grandpa's books.'

Hefring shrugged. It was a small gesture.

'Hefring and her sisters were the billow maidens,' Camilla said excitedly, her eyes lighting up as she spoke. 'That's what the old stories call them. There were nine of them, magical creatures, the daughters of the sea and the storm.'

Hefring chuckled. 'Something like that . . . once upon a time, perhaps . . . My sisters . . . me and my sisters . . . We would spend our days out there, wild and free . . .'

She fell silent, lost in her reverie. Nobody spoke for

a long time. Then the moonlight broke through a thick bank of clouds outside. A silver spear of light darted in through the open doors, illuminating the three of them where they sat. It haloed the strange woman, Hefring. It glinted in her lively eyes and smoothed over her pale body.

'Your skin,' Ailsa said, looking at Hefring's legs.

The sores were healing. They were fully gone in some places. Shiny new skin had taken their place. It shimmered in the moonlight, scaled lightly so that Ailsa thought it looked like it belonged to the fishes that Uncle Nod cooked.

'Aye,' Hefring muttered. 'Aye, so it goes. Your skin, too,' she said, looking at Ailsa.

Ailsa nodded. Her skin was back to normal, the sun's heat and the damage it had caused gone for the moment.

A gentle rain began to patter down outside. It made the moonlight shimmer and dance. The halo flickered around them like dancing flames.

'And on it comes . . .' Hefring whispered, looking out through the open doors to the balcony beyond. Fat raindrops began to splash across the balcony's railing, jumping all around. '. . . That's who I am, who I was . . . the rain, the storm, the wild . . .

'But no more,' she said, snapping out of it. Her head came up and she fixed Ailsa with her glare. 'Now I'm an old fool, the same as every other fool . . . And I'm hungry,' she said, looking pointedly at Ailsa's rucksack, discarded by the door.

'Aye,' Ailsa said. 'I've brought you some things. Sugar and cocoa . . .'

'Like the sailors of old . . .'

'. . . and some real food, to help you get stronger.'

Afterwards, as they left the lighthouse, Camilla sighed deeply. Ailsa led her and Moxie home. The rain continued to fall around them, refreshing and cool after so many days of such intense heat. The hard, baked earth beneath their feet swam with water. Out to sea, high waves crashed and roiled, sounding like their own kind of storm.

'It doesn't seem real,' Camilla said.

'Aye,' Ailsa agreed. 'Maybe. I'm not sure. Sometimes I think of it, and it seems like a dream. Sometimes it seems normal, like the most real thing there could be.'

'Yes, maybe, but it's all so . . . odd,' Camilla said. 'Do you know what I mean?'

Ailsa did. It was all very odd. But then, it had been since she had first stepped into that cave and found the strange woman. No, she thought. It had all been odd since her mum had grown ill and she had had to phone Uncle Nod. It was odd that they were here, on the island, with her mum in bed, a shell of her normal self.

Nothing was normal, she thought. Nothing seemed real at the moment, nothing was as it should be.

So what did a little more oddness matter, on top of all the rest?

'Aye. Maybe,' she said. 'I don't know.'

Fourteen

The rain got heavier through the night and into the following day. The fat, singular drops turned into thin ones that lanced down from the heavens. They turned into sheets of water cascading downwards, washing the world, churning it, drenching and drowning it.

Uncle Nod said it was good. 'About time the fields got some water after all this heat,' he told Ailsa and Aunt Bertha as he stared out at it from the kitchen window. The view was obscured, the yard just about visible as sideways rain lashed against the glass. 'Everything's been browned and burned for so long. It's unnatural up here. I've never seen the like.'

'Aye,' Aunt Bertha mumbled.

The rain got into the earth a little too much, though.

The ground was thirsty. It had drunk when Ailsa and Camilla had walked home from the lighthouse. It drank and it kept drinking until it began to come apart. People reported mudslides all over the island. Ailsa saw a small, rapid stream of mud flowing down the road past Uncle Nod and Aunt Bertha's house.

The subsidence around the cliffs got worse. Whole chunks of cliff face fell down to the beaches below, down into the sea, as the rainwater got into them and pulled them apart. Folks came from the council, wearing bright orange jackets and carrying clipboards. Their truck had thick tyres to churn through the mud. They cordoned off much of the coastline. They cordoned off the route down to the cave.

'The whole stretch is falling apart, apparently,' Uncle Nod said when he arrived back from the yard at lunch time, sopping wet. Ailsa and Aunt Bertha were sitting together at the table, though Aunt Bertha seemed to Ailsa to be distracted by something.

'Some of the caves have fallen in on themselves,' Uncle Nod carried on. 'Big chunks of the cliffs have fallen into the water. Apparently, they dried out too much in all that heat, got weak, and this has started to finish them off.'

Aunt Bertha listened in silence, and then she spoke quietly.

'My love,' she said. 'I think your sister's getting worse.'

Uncle Nod stopped in his tracks. He was halfway out of his sou'wester, dripping in the kitchen doorway, but he froze like a statue as Aunt Bertha's words hit him.

Ailsa sat in silence at the end of the table.

Aunt Bertha looked at her with warm eyes.

'I think perhaps your mum's taken a turn for the worse, hen,' she said. 'She's become less responsive. Even more withdrawn than she was, you know?'

She was right, Ailsa thought. She went up to see her mum. Creeping into her mum's room, the same kind of sadness that she had felt in Hefring's cave welled up all around her. It was like it was coming from her mum, surrounding her, drowning her.

Ailsa stood next to her mum's bed, all alone, that sadness dragging at her.

'Mum,' she whispered. 'Mum,' she said.

Her mum didn't stir. Her cheeks were ashen, and her

eyes were closed. Her eyelids didn't even flicker. She was too far gone, too deep in the sadness, beyond hearing anything in this world.

'Oh, Mum.'

Outside, the rain blackened the sky. Ailsa slumped down next to her mum's bed, fat tears rolling down her cheeks.

She went to see Camilla that evening. Uncle Nod and Aunt Bertha's house was getting too small. The sadness rolling from her mum's room was too much. It threatened to drag them all down.

Camilla was pleased to see her. Ailsa stood in the doorway, shaking water from her coat, stomping it from her wellies.

'Come in, come in,' Camilla said. 'It's horrible out there!'

Camilla's mum and sister were in the living room. The TV was blaring out and her mum kept laughing hysterically.

'Let's go upstairs,' Camilla muttered. They went up and sat in her bedroom.

'How are you doing?' Camilla asked.

'I don't know,' Ailsa replied. 'Mum's worse.'

'Oh. I'm so sorry.'

Ailsa shrugged. 'It happens, like I said. It's not always like this.'

'No?'

'No,' Ailsa said. 'Just sometimes. We usually have lots of fun. It's usually happy. She can be dead silly, my mum.' She thought of Hefring, and she thought of her mum. 'We used to dress up as mermaids quite a bit.'

'What?' Camilla asked.

'Me and Mum would play dress up,' Ailsa told her. 'You know, just for fun, sometimes. For parties, sometimes. Mum really likes Hallowe'en, so we always do something. She used to take me out trick or treating.'

'How lovely.'

'Aye, well,' Ailsa carried on. 'I went through a mermaid phase. A real big one. Me and Mum had to dress up as mermaids all the time. I made us. She bought us costumes online. They squeezed your legs in a bit, for the tail, but our feet would poke out the end so we could sort of . . . waddle . . .'

'Waddle?' Camilla asked, snorting.

'Aye!' Ailsa began to laugh too. 'Aye, we'd go waddling about. She took me to a friend's party when I was about six or seven. Everyone went as princesses. I went as a mermaid. We had to play loads of games and I kept falling over, waddling away, trying to run races and all that in this costume.'

They laughed for a long time. Ailsa mimed it, then Camilla joined in, both of them waddling around her bedroom.

'I feel more like a penguin than a mermaid!' Camilla said.

'Mum said the same thing. But she wore that outfit whenever I asked her to. She said she didn't care how silly she looked. I think she quite liked it, actually. You know, like I said, being silly and that. Just having a laugh.'

'Can you imagine Hefring waddling about like that?' Camilla asked, and they fell about laughing once more.

They sat down on Camilla's bed after a while, and Camilla pulled out a few of her grandfather's books.

'Look at these,' she said, laying them out on her duvet for Ailsa to see.

There was a drawing in one of them of nine beautiful young women with blonde hair and blue eyes. The women were all dressed in pure white robes, all swimming through the ocean. In another, they looked like vicious sea creatures, all bared, sharp teeth, and mean eyes.

'*They are the children of the Norse Lord and Lady of the Seas, Aegir and his wife Ran,*' Camilla read. '*Aeigir and Ran are not gods, like Odin or Thor, nor are they giants, as many falsely believe. They are much older. Aegir's name means simply "the ocean". Ran's means "thief" or "robber". Where Aegir would grant sailors safe passage, Ran would rob their ships, casting her net over them and dragging them down to the deeps, into Aegir's wide jaws.*

'*Aegir and Ran's son is the wind,*' Camilla continued, turning the page, '*though he isn't often spoken about. More often spoken about are their nine daughters, the billow maidens. They are wilful, temperamental spirits who can often be spotted playing in the surf. Much like the mythological mermaids, they call out to sailors and encircle their ships. If they are feeling charitable, they may guide wayward ships to safety, calming the sea and calling out to their brother, the wind, to help fill the ships' sails.*

147

'*If they are feeling rageful or offended, however, the billow maidens can grow violent. They will call up storms and wreck ships, drowning everyone aboard.*'

'Oh,' Ailsa said. She looked at a picture of three of the billow maidens dragging a longboat into the sea. All the sailors were falling into the sea as the billow maidens attacked. She imagined herself in her costume, her mum in her own, waddling along on land, swimming gracefully in the water, as she had always thought they would. She imagined them dragging a longboat through the waves together.

'And look here,' Camilla said. She pointed to a list of names. '*The nine billow maidens are each named for different aspects of the sea. Dufa is the rolling and pitching of the waves . . . Blodughadda is the bloody head of red sea after a battle . . . Byljga is the billowing of waves . . . and look here . . . Hefring is named for the rising tide.*'

Ailsa nodded. Of course she was there. Of course she was one of them. It was all beginning to make sense, of a sort. It was crazy. She couldn't believe she was buying into it. But nothing about Hefring made much sense, or at least no more than any of this.

Ailsa shivered. She felt cold as she looked at the images, cold knowing deep down that one of those billow maidens was Hefring, that she was one of those awful creatures attacking sailors . . . then she remembered Hefring's words.

'Like the sailors of old used to carry . . .'

It was true, all true, and it scared her. The fear curled tightly in her stomach.

'So you really think she's one of them?' Camilla asked.

'Aye, I do,' Ailsa admitted. 'Crazy as it is, silly as it is, I think I do.'

Fifteen

The docks were buzzing the following morning. There was talk that a storm was brewing. Ailsa walked Moxie out along the wharf and the seafront and listened in as all the fishermen gossiped away.

She asked one of them if the coming storm was anything to do with all the rain they had been having. The fisherman laughed good-naturedly.

'No, not that kind of storm, love,' he said. 'A storm of words and maybe worse before the end. The kind of storm that folks make when they're angry, when they've had enough.'

The fishermen were all back from their morning's work. They had their catches, small as they were, and so they stood around, idly smoking and chatting, taking shelter from the rain under the eaves of fishing huts and sheds.

'It's that Galach,' she heard one of them say.

Another man tried to hush him, but a couple of others spat on the floor and swore and agreed with the first man.

'Aye, always the same, isn't it?' they said. 'Rich folk. Stupid toffs, like.'

Ailsa tackled Uncle Nod about it when she and Moxie got back home. 'What was all the fuss about?' she asked him.

'Galach's men,' Uncle Nod replied with a sigh. 'Always them, acting like they own the whole place. Acting like they own everything.'

Ailsa took Moxie out for another wander that afternoon. The falling drizzle cast the whole world into a dark haze. Moxie splashed through puddles and kept stopping to shake himself.

Camilla was up in her tree when Ailsa came back home afterwards. Night was falling. She was wrapped up in waterproofs, staring out towards the sea. A few strands of hair were plastered to her face beneath her hood.

'Hi,' Ailsa called up to her, and Camilla jumped.

Camilla's eyes froze when she looked down at Ailsa. They narrowed and held Ailsa in place. She said:

'If you know a friend you can fully trust,
go often to their house;
grass and brambles grow quickly
upon the untrodden track.'

Then she swallowed hard. Her cheeks flushed pink. 'It's from *Hávamál*,' she told Ailsa. 'Odin said it.'

'Aye? I don't understand it,' Ailsa replied.

Moxie gave himself a hard shake as the rain continued to fall.

Camilla glared, her eyes never wavering. 'Of course you don't,' she snapped. 'I bet you're the same as everyone else. I bet you hate my family, too. It's always the same with you people!'

'What's the matter with you?' Ailsa asked.

'You tell me!'

'I . . . I don't know.'

'Ha!' Camilla clung to a branch and leaned towards

the wall's high top. 'Is there anything you do know, idiot?' she hissed.

'Shut up,' Ailsa said. *'Tosk! Dronning!'*

'Ha! Borrowed words,' Camilla crowed.

'All words are borrowed,' Ailsa replied. 'You borrow them all the time. Speaking in Odin's words, not your own.'

'Shut up!' Camilla snapped. The branch she was holding onto shook.

Ailsa looked closer and saw that Camilla was shaking too, in anger. Ailsa swore at her.

'So you do hate me, then,' Camilla said. She seemed triumphant to Ailsa. She crooned the words. 'Of course you do. You're one of them.'

'One of who?'

'The sheep, the idiots, the normal people,' Camilla snapped. 'And my dad says we're the wolves. And it's normal for us to hunt, he says. We're like Geri and Freki.'

'Hungry, and nothing else,' Ailsa said.

'Strong,' Camilla replied. 'And it's normal for the sheep to hate us.'

'I don't hate you,' Ailsa said. 'I think you're being stupid, but I don't hate you. And I'm not a sheep. But

153

if folks hate you, it's 'cause your dad acts like he owns everything.'

'He does own everything!' Camilla hissed. She wiped her sleeve across her face, smearing tears and rainwater together. 'I suppose you won't let me go with you, any more,' Camilla said.

'Go where?'

'To see Hefring.'

'You can go and see Hefring any time,' Ailsa said. 'You don't need me for that.'

'Is that what you want?' Camilla snapped.

'Don't be so stupid,' Ailsa said.

Camilla dropped from her branch onto the wall. She crouched like a cat, ready to pounce. Ailsa thought she really was going to jump down on top of her. But Camilla stifled a sob, threw her one last dark look, and jumped backwards, out of sight. Ailsa heard her land softly on the other side of the wall.

Ailsa stomped home, her eyes hot and her cheeks burning. She slammed through the kitchen door.

'Ailsa!' Uncle Nod reproved her. He was standing at the sink, scrubbing some dishes.

Aunt Bertha was at the table, filling out the day's crossword. She looked up and frowned. 'What's got into you, then?' she asked.

'Nothing,' Ailsa said. She looked down at the floor. 'Just Camilla being stupid.'

'Aye, well,' Uncle Nod said, softening. 'It must be stressful over there at the moment. Word is the Galachs have had a rough time of it. Nobody's got a good word to say about them. Rightly so, but still, it must be hard on the girls.'

Ailsa shrugged. 'Maybe,' she said. 'Still stupid, though.' She headed up to her room, fuming.

'Ailsa, hen!' Aunt Bertha called up the stairs that evening.

Ailsa popped her head out of her doorway.

'Aye?'

'Someone to see you, my love.'

It was Camilla. She stood just outside the front door in the evening's gloom. Her cheeks were flushed, and she looked at the ground, her hands interlaced and hanging at her waist.

'I invited her in, but she wouldn't come,' Uncle Nod

told Ailsa as she came into the kitchen. 'I think she's a bit embarrassed, love. Go on out, get things settled.'

Ailsa nodded. 'Aye,' she sighed.

Camilla looked up briefly as Ailsa stepped outside. Then she looked back down at her feet.

'They're fighting,' she said.

'Who?' Ailsa asked.

'Mummy and Daddy.'

'Oh. Aye.'

'It's tense.'

'Aye.'

'I'm sorry,' Camilla whispered.

'It's OK.'

'No, but really. I am.'

Camilla snuffled and wiped her nose and her eyes with the cuff of her jacket.

'You OK?' Ailsa asked.

Camilla gasped. Then she sobbed. Then she was crying.

'Oh, Ailsa,' she sighed and fell into Ailsa's arms.

Ailsa held her tight.

'It's just so hard, sometimes, being a Galach,' Camilla said. 'With my family. With my dad. He's so mean, sometimes, and so aggressive, and Mummy just sits around drinking, and I know everyone hates us, and I know why, I know that Daddy's a bully to everyone on the island . . .'

The air was full of the smell of Camilla's wet hair. Her shoulders heaved. Ailsa continued to hold her. She sobbed a few times, then fell still. She straightened and stepped away from Ailsa slightly, placing her hands on Ailsa's shoulders.

'I'm sorry,' she said. 'I know you've got worse problems. With your mum, and all that. It's just that . . . I was finding it hard. I do sometimes.'

'Aye.'

'And I assumed you hated me, because of what my family does, what they are. Everyone hates us.'

'I don't hate you,' Ailsa said. 'And I don't care about your family. I care about you.'

'Can we be friends?'

'We already were, but aye,' Ailsa said.

There was a clattering overhead. Wingbeats cut the air and Camilla flinched as a couple of birds swooped past them, black shadows that were gone quicker than they came.

'I never usually jump at birds,' Camilla said.

Ailsa shrugged. 'Anything can become scary in the dark, can't it?' she said. She came to Camilla's side and took her hand. 'It's OK, though,' she said. 'We're together.'

They held each other's hands tightly as the rain continued to fall.

'I've some cocoa on,' Uncle Nod called out to them. 'If you're interested?'

'Will you come in for a bit?' Ailsa asked Camilla.

'Oh, well . . . Yes please, if that's OK?'

'Aye, come on, then.'

Sixteen

Camilla stayed the night in the end.

'Get some distance, then go back home feeling fresher in the morning,' Aunt Bertha told her.

'Are you sure it's OK?' Camilla asked. Her eyes flickered to the ceiling, beyond which Ailsa's mum slept. 'I know you've got a lot on.'

'Nothing we can't manage,' Uncle Nod interjected. 'And it's always nice to have a house full.'

Uncle Nod called Camilla's house to let them know where she was, and they all stayed sitting around the kitchen table after dinner. The rain was hammering down outside, pinging off the windows, churning into the ground. Though the sun wouldn't set until late, it was already dark. Thick clouds cast everything into twilit shade.

'It's a night for staying in,' Uncle Nod announced as he cleared their plates away.

Ailsa and Camilla had both left the fatty rinds from their cuts, and he tipped their plates with a deft movement of the wrist. The rinds fell to the floor and Moxie was there in a shot, scrabbling to lap it all up.

'We'd best entertain ourselves,' Uncle Nod smiled, dumping everything in the sink. He opened a kitchen drawer, rummaged about and pulled out a deck of cards.

'Anyone for rummy?' he asked.

'Aye, yes please!' Ailsa said.

'I . . . I'm afraid I don't know how to play . . .' Camilla said in a quiet voice.

'Don't worry,' Aunt Bertha said as Uncle Nod sat down and began shuffling cards. 'We'll teach you the basics fast enough. And anyway, Ailsa and Nod are both rubbish. You'll be beating them in no time.'

She winked at Camilla as Uncle Nod and Ailsa both protested, then they all fell about laughing as Uncle Nod began to deal.

'Now,' he said. 'The aim of the game is to go *rummy*.'

'What's that?' Camilla asked.

'You want to get rid of all your cards,' Ailsa said. 'Then you shout "rummy" and you've won, right?'

She looked at Uncle Nod for confirmation, a little unsure. She only ever played rummy at their house, and it had been quite a long time since her last game.

'Aye, that's about it,' Uncle Nod said. 'Though you can go out without being rummy.'

'Don't overcomplicate things, love,' Aunt Bertha told him, and he shrugged.

'They're smart girls,' he said. 'We can do it right. Anyway, get rid of all your cards and you win.'

He carried on dealing as Aunt Bertha got up and fetched a few glasses. She poured cold cola from the fridge into two of them for Ailsa and Camilla. Then she opened a cabinet set high on the wall and pulled out a half-drunk bottle of whiskey. She poured a small amount into her and Uncle Nod's glasses, set them all down, and sat back heavily in her chair.

'It's not cards without a bit of a tipple,' she said.

Uncle Nod laughed.

'Now,' he told Camilla, dishing out the last couple of cards. They each had seven cards face down before them.

'We all want to form matched sets, groups of three or four cards from the same group. They can be in order, from the same suit . . . you know, two, three, four, five, or ten, jack, queen. Or they can be three or four of a kind . . . three threes, three jacks, four eights, that kind of thing. Make sense?'

'I think so,' Camilla said, though Ailsa could see she wasn't too sure.

'You pick up a new card every turn, you get rid of one in the middle, or simply throw your new card away. When you've got your three or four to lay down, you put them in the middle. Get rid of all your cards and you win.

'Easy peasy,' he finished, grinning at Camilla.

Camilla lost the first game. She didn't really work out what was going on until near the end, by which time everyone else was too far ahead. Ailsa ended up winning.

She won the second game, though. Then Aunt Bertha won, then Camilla won again, cheering loudly. Any sadness emanating from Ailsa's mum's room was banished for the moment. Everybody laughed pretty much constantly.

Everybody except for Uncle Nod, that is, who kept losing.

'Beginner's luck,' he harrumphed, finishing his glass of whiskey and going to pour himself and Aunt Bertha another one. 'Let's see if it holds. One more game before bed?'

Everyone agreed. Camilla won, squealing with delight as she laid down the last of her cards. Uncle Nod still had a full hand.

'Crikey, you've a good head on your shoulders, lass,' he told her, shaking his head and looking resigned.

Camilla blushed deep crimson and beamed.

It was true night outside by the time they finished. The sun went down around half past ten. The clouds and the rain swallowed any moonlight so that the windows were completely black. Uncle Nod yawned and stretched his arms, his joints cracking and popping as he did so.

'Time for bed,' Aunt Bertha said. 'For all of us, I think.'

Ailsa and Camilla sat up talking for a little while when they went to bed, wrapped up in the duvet.

'Your aunt and uncle's house is so much nicer than mine,' Camilla said.

'What?' Ailsa asked, incredulous. 'What are you

talking about? Your house is amazing. It's massive and beautiful. I mean, it's got its own wall and big gates and everything.'

'Yes, but . . . well, it's big, but it's cold. It's beautiful – it *should* be beautiful . . . but it's so hard, and my parents are always fighting, and my dad isn't always the nicest to be around, especially when he's stressed. This house, though,' Camilla sighed, looking all around. 'It's warm, it's comfortable and cosy, it's full of love. Even with your mum, you know . . . with her not being well and everything, it's still a very happy place. So it's much nicer.'

'Aye, well, you're always welcome here,' Ailsa said. 'Even after I go back home, I reckon. Uncle Nod and Aunt Bertha would love it if you popped in for a cuppa sometimes. You know, when you're not living at your posh school and all that.'

Camilla laughed at the thought. Ailsa laughed too.

'Even when I'm such a beast?' Camilla asked quietly when they stopped laughing. 'Even with my family, you know . . . not being the nicest people.'

Ailsa shrugged.

'I already told you, that doesn't mean much,' she said.

'You're my friend, no matter what your family does. No matter what they are. No matter if you get stressed out sometimes. We all do.'

Camilla put her arms around Ailsa, then. She cried softly, but only for a minute or so.

'You'll always be welcome round here,' Ailsa told her as they lay down and pulled the duvet around themselves.

'Thank you, Ailsa,' Camilla whispered. 'Thank you.'

Ailsa dreamed once more that her mum was drowning. They were standing together on the clifftops as the rain fell hard. Lightning flashed across the sky and thunder boomed. The cliffs began to crumble and both she and her mum fell.

The sea caught them, churning as Ailsa kicked out hard, trying to stay afloat. Her mum kicked too, though she wasn't strong enough. She grew tired and her legs grew heavy. She lay still and the waves covered her, pulling her down.

'Mum!' Ailsa gasped, sitting up in bed.

Moxie jumped up, his forepaws on the bed beside her. Camilla stirred, mumbling, before sitting up.

'Are you OK, Ailsa?' she asked.

Far off, thunder and lightning whispered at the horizon, out across the broad sea. Rainwater pattered against the windowpane. Ailsa thought she could hear the sound of singing beneath it, low and sweet and almost beyond telling.

Moxie tried to lick her face, but she stopped him.

'I think we need to go to Hefring,' she said. The fear she had felt towards the billow maidens died suddenly. Now she just felt an overwhelming need to go to the lighthouse.

Moxie wagged his tail and gave a little, low whine.

Camilla nodded. 'Yes, I think you're right,' she said, gazing out of the window. She was sweating, too.

Ailsa's mum's door was ajar. She poked her head inside on her way past. Everything was dark and quiet. Her mum's gentle breathing was quiet, barely audible.

She put her wellies and coat on by the kitchen door as Camilla pulled her own trainers on. Then they hurried onwards, through the night, with Moxie ranging ahead of them. There were a couple of dark cars parked outside the Galachs' house. A man stood by the gate, glaring outwards, though he didn't see them go past.

The rain fell hard, and they ran. It was the first time Ailsa had left to visit Hefring at night without being at all scared, though she only realised it as they drew close to the finger of rock leading across to the lighthouse.

They were both soaked through by the time they got there. The smell of saltwater and dampness greeted Ailsa and Camilla as they entered the lighthouse. There was something else, too, another smell layered below it. It was indefinable, something cold and almost metallic.

'Look,' Camilla breathed, pointing.

The walls were shimmering. Algae or moss was growing in faint lines along them. It seemed to sparkle silvery blue. Crystals clung to the skirting boards and bannisters, to the floor at the edges.

'Stalagmites,' Camilla breathed. She looked up to the ceiling and the doors. 'Stalactites, look!' she said.

They were forming in the doorframes, pointing downwards, and in the cornices around the ceiling's edges, all small and pale.

'But how could they form so fast?' she asked.

Ailsa shrugged. 'Who knows anything with Hefring?' she replied.

The stairs creaked as they climbed them. Dampness clung to them. It sucked at their feet. Upstairs, they found the balcony doors flung open. Sea spray misted the air, blown in on a cold wind.

Hefring was standing out on the balcony, arms spread wide, her skin bare to the night and the salt spray. Pale moonlight flickered through the falling rain, outlining her silhouette as she gazed out to sea. It radiated through the room, seemingly coming as much from the walls themselves as the night sky outside.

Hefring turned as they came towards her. Though her skin was still as haggard looking as ever, and though her hair was as lank and her face as ravaged with age as ever, Ailsa thought that she walked with confidence. Though still bloody and raw, and though she limped slightly, her feet were nevertheless well-planted as she stood before them.

She nodded, as though reading Ailsa's thoughts.

'I am beginning to remember my old strength, I think,' she said. Her voice was not as thin as it had been before. There was a richness to it, as though she could command the waves themselves with its power.

'Come here, little one,' she said to Ailsa. 'Come, little *dronning*,' she said to Camilla.

Camilla and Moxie moved forwards. Ailsa hesitated.

'Come, come,' Hefring repeated. 'There is something I wanted to show you.'

Ailsa moved. Camilla took her hand and Hefring led them out onto the balcony. The wind buffeted them as it came in over the sea. The air was thick with spray and rain. Ailsa crunched something beneath her boot and looked down. The balcony was littered with fish bones.

Camilla squeezed Ailsa's hand. Moxie stood at her other side, and she took the fur between his shoulders in her closed fist, holding on.

'Listen,' Hefring said.

The smell of dead things wafted from her as she stepped ahead of them to the balcony's railing. It was a dockyard stench of rotten fish, of guts and flesh.

'Listen,' Hefring repeated, closing her eyes and raising her arms out to the side. The clouds parted overhead. The moonlight brightened. It broke on the water below. It broke on their faces, lighting Camilla's features, lighting her wide eyes and broad smile. The waves rushed and whirled down below, crashing against the rocks.

Then Hefring began to sing, and all time seemed to halt. The world seemed to hold its breath.

Ailsa closed her eyes to listen. It was like no human voice. It shimmered and it danced, almost visible in its liveliness. It tinkled like tiny bells one moment, before ringing loud the next. It was faint and powerful at once. Rage and peace were held in its notes, as were joy and sadness, order and madness, and everything in between. It was Hefring's song, and it was the song of the sea. The shallows of sunlit rock pools and trickling brooks ran through it. The deep wilderness of the ocean boomed through it, mile high waves and crashing storms were encompassed within its notes.

Ailsa imagined that she could hear the whole world in that moment. She felt its terrible age, its aeons of life as it spun and spun, life growing and dying and growing anew on its surface. She could also feel it as it was when it was young, before lighthouses were built and ships plied the seas. Before people stood tall and walked its face. It was fresh, bursting with new life, untested and untamed.

It made her think of her mum. It held sadness, such awful sadness in it that it could crush you. But there was strength there too, and joy, sometimes, and laughter as often as tears, life as much as death. It had all things in it, just like her mum did.

Opening her eyes again, Ailsa saw the same sea that had churned for millennia, and she found herself crying. Camilla was crying next to her, and Moxie had his nose to the air, a look of bliss across his features.

The song faded. Its last notes stretched out until a single, lovely breath glistened around the balcony.

'Don't stop, please,' Ailsa said.

Hefring allowed her arms to fall to her sides. She turned.

'All things end, little one,' she said. 'But all things begin again, reborn from what once was.'

'What was that?' Camilla asked.

'The next part in the longest song,' Hefring replied. She smiled sadly to herself. 'Too long absent from these shores, I'd wager,' she said.

'It's beautiful,' Camilla said.

'It's dying, isn't it?' Ailsa asked. 'The song?'

Hefring nodded. Then she shrugged. 'Aye,' she agreed. 'As I said, all things end. It's the shape of tomorrow that matters. It's whether we can find a few more notes, a few more days lived, that matters.'

'Can we?' Ailsa asked. 'Can you?'

'Oh, aye,' Hefring said. 'Always. Always, always . . . but I'll need your help . . . little ones.'

'Anything,' Camilla said.

'Aye,' Ailsa said.

Hefring nodded. 'Thank you,' she sighed. She was tired. She swayed on the spot and Camilla took her arm, supporting her.

'But not yet . . . soon . . .' she whispered. Her voice was hoarse once more. Then she licked her lips with a dry tongue. 'Did you bring any . . . sugar and cocoa . . . ?' she asked.

Seventeen

They spent the next day sheltering from the rain in Camilla's house. Camilla took Ailsa up into the loft to see her grandad's old things.

'It's like a pirate's treasure trove up there,' she said. She pulled a ladder down from the loft hatch, climbed it and pushed the hatch open.

Ailsa followed as Camilla flicked a light on.

There was a layer of thick dust over almost everything. Old boxes and pieces of furniture lay all about. Cobwebs clung to everything. The only things that looked like they had been moved recently were a few cardboard packing boxes and a couple of large trunks propped up in one corner.

'Come and see,' Camilla said, leading Ailsa over to them.

'What's in them?' Ailsa asked.

Camilla threw one of the trunks open. There was a collection of old things inside. A sailor's uniform lay folded at the bottom. A telescope and a couple of diaries nestled into it, as did a large, folded map that Ailsa could see had rings drawn onto it in red ink.

'From when he was a sailor, before he started the business,' Camilla told her. She pulled out the map. The rings were all over it, on every continent.

'He marked down all the places he ever went so he wouldn't forget,' Camilla said.

'Wow,' Ailsa said. She nodded at the other trunk. It was sturdier than the first, coated in thick leather, with iron bands around its edges. A couple of large padlocks kept it locked tight. 'What's in that one?' she asked.

'I don't know,' Camilla replied. 'Daddy won't open it for me. He said I have to wait until I leave school and join the business.'

'Oh.'

'But forget that,' Camilla said. She opened one of the old cardboard packing boxes. What must have been fifty or more books were tightly crammed inside. 'This is the real treasure,' she said.

She began to pull out books at random. 'They're all on mythology,' Camilla said. 'Practically all on Norse and Celtic mythology. He was obsessed.'

'So are you,' Ailsa said, and Camilla grinned at her.

'Come on, let's try this one,' Camilla said, picking one. The cover was a picture of a stylised raven spreading its wings.

'We've already looked at the ravens,' Ailsa protested.

'There's so much more to them than just Huginn and Muninn,' Camilla said. 'They crop up all over the place. Come on, let me show you.'

They took it down to Camilla's bedroom, propped it open against a cushion and both sat on the floor, looking at the pictures.

'Ravens are special because they exist between life and death,' Camilla told Ailsa. 'They're carrion birds, you see. That means they find and eat dead bodies . . .' She read from the book, skimming the lines as she spoke. 'This book says this *makes them a mediator between the living and the dead.*

'And here, look,' she said, pointing to another page. 'In German folklore, they are the ghosts of people with damned souls. In Sweden, they say they are the ghosts of people who haven't been properly buried.'

'Aye?' Ailsa asked.

'Yes, and in the Greek myths, they brought bad luck and they were the god Apollo's messengers in the mortal world.'

'Like the Norse?' Ailsa asked. 'The same as Odin?'

'I guess so. Apollo was the god of the sun and of reason and logic. He used them to spy on people.'

'Funny that.'

'Yes, well,' Camilla said. 'It doesn't end there.'

'Oh?'

'They gave Apollo bad news one day,' Camilla told her, pointing to one picture. There were a couple of white birds flying into the heavens. 'They told him that his girlfriend had cheated on him, so he set them on fire and scorched them black.'

There was a man in the picture. He wore a toga and a crown of flowers. He held his hand out and the white birds burned black.

'Ravens have been black ever since,' Camilla said. She turned a page and Ailsa saw a picture of Noah's Ark.

'In the Bible, Noah sent one out into the great flood to find land.'

'I thought that was a dove,' Ailsa said.

'Eventually, Noah sent out a dove. But first he sent a raven. It didn't come back, though. Probably because it was eating the bodies of the people who had drowned in the flood. It couldn't find dry land, either way, so people think that ravens are the bringers of bad news.'

'Oh,' Ailsa said.

There was a knock at the door.

'Go away, Suzanne!' Camilla shouted.

'It's me,' Camilla's mum said from the other side. She opened the door. She looked tired and took a second to focus as she eyed Ailsa.

'It's your aunt,' she said. 'She's downstairs.'

Aunt Bertha was at the foot of the staircase.

'What's happened?' Ailsa asked as she bolted down the stairs.

'It's your mum, hen,' Aunt Bertha said. Her voice was hushed. 'She's not doing so well. Your Uncle Nod's taken her to the hospital on the mainland to see the doctors there.'

Suzanne stood in the door to the living room, holding a half-eaten orange. She frowned and licked some juice from her thumb.

'Is it her head or her heart?' she asked simply. 'I heard it was one of them.'

Camilla gasped and Mrs Galach began to shush Suzanne and apologise to Aunt Bertha. Aunt Bertha waved her away, though. She turned to Suzanne with a sad smile on her face.

'It's probably a bit of both, sweetheart,' she told her. 'Most likely a bit of both.'

Ailsa left with Aunt Bertha. She was shaking and she could feel tears beginning to sting behind her eyes. As they made their way home, she saw a dark bird swooping high overhead and she imagined it was a raven, caught between life and death, telling tales to the gods above.

Moxie came charging over to them as they got to their own front garden. He leaped up, put his great paws on Ailsa's shoulders and began to lick her face. His sharp dog breath made her wrinkle her nose and his fur was wet, but she held onto him.

Eighteen

Aunt Bertha wanted to keep busy the following morning. She wanted to keep Ailsa busy, too.

'Come on,' she said. 'You can help me bring some bits up from the docks to the yard.'

They drove down to the docks as a light rain pattered against the windscreen and loaded the truck with some boxes from one of the big sheds. The sky darkened as they drove home. Black clouds gathered, shutting out the sunlight, and the rain grew heavier. From one second to the next, it seemed to grow from a slight drizzle to a torrent, beating down at them. Back at the yard, they both got soaked as they began to unload everything into a couple of wheelbarrows. Mud ran in filthy streams all around them.

Aunt Bertha cursed. Ailsa slipped in the mud and the rain clattered against her head and shoulders. First, she skidded a few feet. Then her feet went out from under her, and she tumbled backwards, falling onto her behind. Her wheelbarrow tipped to the side and spilled its contents.

'Ha! Oh my!' Aunt Bertha cried as Ailsa slid to a stop beside her. She bent over, her own feet steady, and shook with laughter.

'It's not funny!' Ailsa shouted. She tried to get to her feet, slipped once more, then managed to find her feet and stand. Mud clung to her, dripping from her legs, back, arms and hands.

Aunt Bertha continued to chuckle to herself. Ailsa's face grew hot. She balled her fists as her heart hammered in her chest.

'I told you it wasn't funny!' she screamed at Aunt Bertha. Then she began to swear. She used all the swear words she knew in a tirade as everything seemed to well up inside her.

The laughter stopped at once. Aunt Bertha turned red. Her eyes went cold.

'Now, listen here, young lady,' she said. 'Don't you dare talk to me like that. Don't you dare use such filthy language—'

'I told you it wasn't funny, and you laughed!' Ailsa shouted. She stood firm. 'You laughed and laughed. And I'm wet and dirty and stuck in this horrible place with this horrible mud when I should be at home, in my own home, with my mum . . .'

Before she knew it, Ailsa was on her knees in the wet yard. Great, hot tears welled in her eyes and began to run down her cheeks as her shoulders heaved. She sobbed and she sobbed as her tears mixed with the rainwater. It felt good to get it all out, everything that had been building up inside her. It felt good to rage and scream, then to weep, to weep until her eyes stung and her throat was sore.

The rain crashed down all around them, churning the world to sludge. It bounced from Aunt Bertha's shoulders as she stood over Ailsa.

'Oh, my dear sweetheart,' Aunt Bertha said. There was such warmth in her voice that the downpour seemed to Ailsa to lessen slightly. Aunt Bertha kneeled down in front of Ailsa, in the mud, and she put her hands on Ailsa's shoulders.

'You're not alone, hen,' she said. There was no trace of anger left in her. There was only sadness and worry.

'There's plenty of us yet who love you to death,' she said. 'Me. Your Uncle Nod. Even Moxie too, I'd say, maybe more than anyone. We've always been there for you, and we always will be. We might be having to look out for you a bit more than normal for the moment, but your mum'll get better again soon enough. She always does, in the end. And, in the meantime, we get to spend all this extra time together.'

She looked around ruefully at the rain and the mud. 'Such as it is, of course,' she said.

'Aye,' Ailsa muttered. She began to shake. It was hard to stop now that it was all coming out, and she carried on sobbing for some time.

Aunt Bertha put her arms around her and pulled her in tight. They were both entirely sodden, both sunk into the running filth, but they clung to one another in place, nonetheless.

'Now,' Aunt Bertha said eventually. 'Let's get this lot put

away and head back indoors, aye? I'll put some hot chocolate on, and we can get changed out of these wet things.'

'Aye,' Ailsa said. She nodded and wiped her nose and eyes on her sleeve. 'Aye.'

Camilla came to the house not long after they got home. The rain had abated for the moment, though the clouds were still thick overhead. A warm breeze stirred the world.

'Look who it is,' Aunt Bertha said. She was at the kitchen sink, warm and dry now, rinsing out the finished mugs of hot chocolate. She watched Camilla as she came up the garden path. 'A real pal you've found for yourself, there, eh?' she said.

'Aye,' Ailsa agreed.

Aunt Bertha was right, she thought. Camilla was a proper friend, probably the best Ailsa had ever had.

'I'll leave you two to it, then,' Aunt Bertha said. She cleared off to the garage. The sound of hammering duly started up as she began to work on something or another.

The door was ajar, and Camilla let herself in.

'I came to see how you were doing,' she said. 'I saw your truck pulling up outside the yard.'

Ailsa nodded.

'Well?' Camilla asked.

'Well, what?'

'How are you doing?' Camilla smiled and came to sit at the kitchen table, opposite Ailsa.

'I'm OK,' Ailsa replied.

'No, you're not,' Camilla said. 'Of course you're not. Have you heard anything?'

'Aye,' Ailsa said. 'Aunt Bertha heard from Uncle Nod this morning. I spoke to him, too.'

'And?'

Ailsa shrugged. 'Mum's been put on some stronger drugs,' she said. 'I suppose they'll turn her into even more of a zombie.'

'Is that what they do?' Camilla asked.

Ailsa nodded. 'Aye,' she grumbled. 'They're meant to keep her safe, but they're worse than anything else, I reckon. They shut her down. Turn her into some kind of robot or something.'

'That's awful.'

'Aye.'

'Hefring says your mum needs to relearn her song,' Camilla said. 'Like the song she showed us, you know?'

'Hefring? You went to see her?'

'Yes,' Camilla said. 'I was worried last night. I slept badly, then I thought I heard her song. I *did* hear her song . . . I think. It was faint, rolling in off the sea, and I followed it again. I went early this morning, took her a flask of hot chocolate and some different bits of food.'

'Aye.'

'She said your mum is more than she appears right now—' Camilla began, but Ailsa cut her off.

'I know,' she said. 'I've felt it.'

Her mum was sad and sick, but she was joyful and strong, too, sometimes . . . she looked like death, but there was so much life in her most of the time that it would almost burst from her. Ailsa knew it from watching her. She knew it from listening to Hefring's song, though she couldn't quite explain it.

'Hefring said the world isn't done with your mum, even if she thinks she's done with it,' Camilla carried on.

185

'She said she would sing for her, and her soul would wake up again. She said there's a lot of strength left.'

'Aye, I know,' Ailsa said.

'I'm worried, though,' Camilla carried on, frowning. 'About Hefring. About the lighthouse. You should see it. I went scuba diving in some reefs in Malta last summer. It's beginning to look like that. Shells and plants and damp growing up everywhere.' She shrugged, looking puzzled. 'I asked her about it, but she just told me to go away and get her some more chocolate.'

Camilla giggled, then she laughed properly. Her eyes flashed and Ailsa found herself smiling. Then she began to laugh, too. Soon enough, tears were rolling down both their cheeks as she and Camilla split their sides laughing.

The door opened and Mrs Tomlinson backed in, carrying a large wicker hamper. 'Well, it's good to hear some merriment,' she said. She shot Camilla a funny look, though it passed quickly, and then she was all smiles again.

'Give me a hand with this, Ailsa, love,' she said.

Ailsa got up and hurried over to take the hamper. It was heavy and she was surprised at how easily Mrs

186

Tomlinson had been carrying it. She braced her legs and heaved, just about managing to take it to the kitchen counter, dumping it there with a thud.

'Any news?' Mrs Tomlinson asked. 'Are your aunt and uncle about, and how's your poor mama getting on?' Another spate of hammering came from the garage and Mrs Tomlinson smiled. 'Someone's at home, at least, then?'

'Aye,' Ailsa said. 'Aunt Bertha. She's taking me over to see Mum in a bit. Uncle Nod's there now. They've put Mum on some stronger pills, and they're keeping her under observation.'

'Aye, good,' Mrs Tomlinson said. 'They'll see her right.'

'What's in the hamper, Mrs Tomlinson?' Camilla asked.

'Oh, you know, just some bits and pieces,' Mrs Tomlinson replied. 'Homemade bread and jam. Fresh eggs from my coop. Some soup and a couple of casseroles.' She looked at Ailsa and smiled and winked. 'And some chocolate cake and some more brownies, of course. We've all got to be naughty, sometimes, don't we?'

'Fantastic,' Ailsa said. She shared a look with Camilla and they both smiled.

Mrs Tomlinson looked Ailsa up and down. 'The aloe worked, then?' she asked. 'And the poor weather of late too, I suppose. It's hard to keep up a bad sunburn with rain like we've been having.'

'Aye,' Ailsa said. 'The aloe worked really well.'

Aunt Bertha drove Ailsa to the hospital that afternoon. Some of the roads were flooded so they had to take a bit of a winding route to the ferry. The crossing itself was a little choppy. Ailsa stood at the ferry's prow once more, right at the front, breathing in the sea air as they churned their way across the water.

Aunt Bertha sat in the truck, parked up in the ferry's rear. 'Blow that, in all this rain,' she muttered, and stayed put.

The rain did indeed spatter down all around as Ailsa leaned into the wind. She was the only person out on the deck, and she raised her arms up by her sides. She imagined she was Hefring, singing aloud with the sounds of the ocean. She imagined she was singing to her mum, filling her mum up with it all, waking her up and making her well again.

It wasn't to be, of course. The ferry docked, she had to get back in the truck, and they drove off. The windscreen wipers squeaked, and Aunt Bertha glared at the road, winding around the coast and then inland until they came to the hospital. It was a bit of a drive, but the roads weren't flooded here so they made good time.

The hospital itself was a small building. In the city where Ailsa lived, she was used to seeing hospitals the size of small towns. This was just a couple of blocks, neither more than a couple of storeys high. It was sad looking and dreary. The grey skies and falling rain seemed to Ailsa to suit it very well.

Uncle Nod met them in the car park. He bundled Ailsa into a deep hug, pulling her in tight and squeezing hard.

'Uncle Nod!' Ailsa moaned at first, trying to push herself away.

'Don't be so foolish, my love,' Uncle Nod replied, and Ailsa sank into his arms. He smelled of sweat and paint and oil. She smiled despite herself, comforted and safe.

Uncle Nod led them into the larger of the hospital's two buildings, past a reception desk and up a flight of stairs. Ailsa's mum was in a ward off a surprisingly bright, airy corridor. She was asleep when they arrived. Her hair was sweaty and plastered to her pillow. Her skin looked grey and thin.

'Go on, sit down, say hello, hen,' Aunt Bertha told Ailsa.

There was a plastic chair next to her mum's bed and Ailsa sat down on it quietly. Uncle Nod went to her mum's other side and stared down at her. He took off his cap and held it to his chest and blinked hard and slow as his eyes grew watery.

Her mum lay completely still. There were sturdy cuffs attached to her bed. They were open and loose, flopped down against the side of the bed, though Ailsa noticed that the woman in the next bed over had her cuffs closed over her wrists. She lay smiling at the ceiling, silently whispering something over and over.

Dr Arbuthnot was standing in the corner of the ward. There were three other beds in the ward and Ailsa didn't see him at first. He was reading a chart and nodding his head when she noticed him. He looked up and smiled at her.

'We have her on an increased dose of sertraline, as well as some powerful sedatives,' he told Aunt Bertha. He seemed to glide over to them. He spoke slowly, in a low, precise tone.

'What does that mean? She's OK?' Aunt Bertha asked.

'Yes, for the moment,' Dr Arbuthnot said. 'Though I would like a word. In private,' he said, looking pointedly at Ailsa.

'Aye, OK then,' Aunt Bertha replied. She and Uncle Nod followed Dr Arbuthnot out into the corridor.

Ailsa watched them go. She watched them gather together and whisper opposite the open door. Her aunt and uncle looked anxious. Dr Arbuthnot looked sombre. He kept looking down at his chart.

The woman murmuring at the ceiling made a little noise. She mumbled and groaned, then fell silent once more.

It's no song, Ailsa thought.

Nineteen

Camilla was right about the lighthouse. It looked as though a great reef was taking over. As Ailsa stood outside with her and Moxie, she saw that the front door was warping slightly. It was bowing outwards, like whatever was inside could barely be contained. Lichen clung to the insides of the window and slick moss climbed the front steps. Stepping inside, pushing through the damp front door, felt like stepping into an underwater cavern. The light was dappled and tinged a pallid greenish blue as it filtered through the windows. Sandy residue had collected in the corners of the floor and scuttling crabs rattled through the shadows.

They found Hefring upstairs, as usual. The balcony doors were closed. She was in the middle of the room, sitting cross legged on the floor. Her eyes were closed. Her skin was pale. She looked almost as ragged as when Ailsa had first found her.

Ailsa rushed over to her with Moxie and Camilla just behind her. They all crouched down around Hefring, though Hefring's eyes barely seemed to flutter.

'Hefring!' Ailsa whispered urgently.

'Hello . . . little one,' Hefring croaked. Her voice was weak and thin.

'What happened? What's wrong?' Ailsa asked.

'Age and foolishness . . . the same as happens to us all,' Hefring murmured. 'Old mistakes . . . coming home to roost . . .'

'But you were doing so well,' Ailsa said. 'You were getting so much stronger.'

Hefring shrugged. Her eyelids flickered open, though her gaze was unfocused. 'I rallied, is all,' she said. 'Temporary . . . fleeting . . . but the flesh is weak . . . this flesh is weak,' she sighed, gesturing clumsily to her legs.

Hefring pointed to the little tin mug. It sat nearby, filled with water. Ailsa picked it up and helped Hefring to drink. Then Hefring nodded to a little pile of food. Ailsa took out a half-eaten bar of chocolate, broke it into small chunks and held them out. Hefring took a couple of pieces and popped them into her mouth, closing her eyes with pleasure as she chewed and swallowed.

'That's better,' she said. 'Much better.'

She looked up at Ailsa. 'How's your mamma, then?' she asked. 'Still shut up . . . still cut off from her song . . . ? You're so young . . . too young for the burden . . . too young to know of such things . . .'

She took a deep breath.

'You have heard my song,' she said, meeting Ailsa's eyes. There was a sense of urgency in Hefring's gaze that Ailsa had never seen before. 'I have opened my heart and you have felt it. You have felt the world responding to it, and my song, in turn, responding to the world.'

'Yes,' Ailsa whispered.

'We all need to listen and to sing,' Hefring said. 'It's the only way. There is life in the song. If you forget how to listen to it, you will fade. There is no hope left. If you re-learn what we all once knew, what children know, what animals know,' she said, smiling at Ailsa, Camilla and Moxie in turn, 'then the hope comes back.

'Your mamma needs to listen to the world's song,' Hefring said. 'And she needs to remember how to sing her own, in her own way. That will never happen while we are trapped, cooped up, forced to sit still when all we want to do is run and dance and swim.

'Life,' she sighed, her eyes once more in Ailsa's. 'Life is the answer. We can only live it if we are strong. And we can only be strong if we live it. Do you understand?'

'I . . . I think so,' Ailsa said. She wasn't sure that it made complete sense, but she thought she knew what Hefring was talking about.

'But then why aren't you . . . you know, strong?' she asked. 'Why are you fading, when your song is so beautiful?'

Hefring chuckled to herself. It caught in her throat and she choked. She coughed and spluttered until Ailsa held up another cup of water for her. She drank a few sips and relaxed, lying still.

'I am incomplete,' she said. 'A part of me is missing. Without it . . . well, you can only hope for so long . . .'

'What part?' Camilla asked.

'An important part . . .' Hefring said, gazing down at her raw legs.

'Is there anything we can do?' Ailsa asked.

Hefring looked sad. She looked reluctant to speak. Finally, she nodded.

'There is,' she said.

'What is it?'

'You can . . . listen,' Hefring said, 'to a story.'

'A story?' Camilla asked, incredulous.

'Aye, a story . . . where all the best magic happens,' Hefring said. 'You of all people should know that, little *dronning*.'

'What story?' Ailsa asked.

'Aye, well, it's an old one,' Hefring said. 'Old and sad, like all the best stories are.'

She sat up a little straighter as she began. 'It's about selkies, as foolish men call them. Or one particular selkie, at least. A creature of the sea. A creature of myth. Like all selkies, she could turn human by shedding her sea-skin. At sea, she swam as strong as any whale. On land, she danced as lightly as any child.

'One day, she met a man, whom she took as her lover. He was a bad man with a wicked spirit. The selkie knew it, perhaps, but it didn't stop her. Something about him drew her to him. But she quickly saw her error . . . she saw his wicked ways and decided she would leave.

'The man was as cunning as he was mean, however. He had no love for the selkie, not really. He was in love with her power, the power she held over the sea. He stole her sea-skin before she could go. Once a selkie's sea-skin has been stolen, she is trapped on land and bound to whomever stole it until she can get it back.

'The selkie would not be bound, however. Though she could not retrieve her sea-skin, and though she could not return to the sea, she refused to stay captive to the wicked man. So, one black night when there was no moon and the stars were all hidden behind clouds, she fled. She hid.

'The selkie knew she would die eventually. Without their sea-skin and the ocean's strength flowing through them, selkies do not last. The world of man is no good for such a creature. It serves only to diminish them.'

'What happened?' Camilla asked.

'Exactly that,' Hefring replied. 'The man kept her skin and she crept away, broken and powerless, to hide away and die.'

'But she didn't die,' Ailsa said. 'It's you, isn't it?'

'Of course,' Hefring said simply.

'That's what happened to you?' Camilla asked, horrified.

'Aye,' Hefring replied. A single tear broke from under her closed eyelid and carved a lonely path down her cheek.

'Who was he, this man?' Ailsa asked.

Hefring sighed, long and low. She opened her eyes, though she looked down at the floor.

'A man who was young a long time ago by your reckoning,' she said. 'Who died and left everything he had to his eldest son, as men do.'

She looked up at Camilla. The sadness had returned, the utter heartbreak that Ailsa had felt when she first ever met her.

'His name was Peter,' Hefring said. 'He was a young sailor from these parts. Handsome and headstrong, clever and wicked . . . Peter Galach.'

Camilla gasped. 'My grandpa,' she whispered.

Hefring nodded.

'Aye,' she said. 'It was your grandpa, child. Before he made his fortune. Before he met your grandma and started his family. It's how he became so successful. It's

198

how he mastered the sea, such as a man can do. He kept my sea-skin and his family . . . your family . . . have held onto its power ever since. I told you I knew your family of old.'

'But he died,' Camilla said. 'A boating accident when I was a girl.'

Hefring nodded. She smiled slightly. 'Aye, the sea can never be completely tamed,' she whispered to herself. Her teeth looked sharp. Her eyes glinted. 'And now your father has it,' she said, looking at Camilla once more.

'How can you know that?' Ailsa asked.

'I feel it, girl,' Hefring said. She closed her eyes and took a deep breath, looking peaceful for a long moment. 'It's close by. It calls to me, locked deep inside the mansion that Peter Galach built.'

'My house?' Camilla asked. 'It's in my house?'

'Where else?' Hefring asked. 'Locked away, the Galach family's most treasured possession, the fount of all their wealth.'

'In that case . . . I think I may know where it is,' Ailsa said. Her heart pounded. She found herself shaking in excitement, riled up in a way she didn't usually feel. But

199

this was perfect! She and Camilla could actually fix it all. They might finally be able to properly help Hefring.

'What?' Camilla asked.

'I think I know where it is,' Ailsa repeated, trying to stay calm. 'In your house, you know. Your grandpa's stuff in the loft. It's the old trunk, the padlocked one. It's got to be. Your dad's never let you open it up. It's the only thing up there you've not been allowed to go through, and it's locked up tight like your dad's afraid to let anyone into it.'

'Yes, I think you might be right,' Camilla said.

'Do you think we could get into it?' Ailsa asked.

Camilla took a little while to answer. Her face was pale and drawn. She quivered slightly as she looked at Hefring. Her hands were shaking. Then she looked at Ailsa. Ailsa saw the shock in her eyes. She saw the fear and the disbelief at the situation.

As their eyes locked, Camilla gave Ailsa the briefest of shakes of her head.

No, it seemed to say. *No, this is too much . . . no, I can't do this . . . no, I don't want this to be happening . . .*

'Camilla,' Ailsa whispered. 'Camilla, this is important . . .'

Camilla's eyes still stood out, bright and shining. Their whites were wide and they had tears in them, fat tears ready to drop because, Ailsa realised, it was all too much for her. It had all become too real all of a sudden.

Finally, just as Ailsa was about to speak, to try to convince Camilla, Camilla nodded.

'I . . . I think so,' she said in a very small voice.

'Camilla, it's important,' Ailsa said.

'I know, I know,' Camilla replied. She cleared her throat. She looked away from Ailsa and brushed the tears from her eyes.

'Yes . . .' she said. It seemed to Ailsa as though she were trying to make her voice sound firm and certain. 'Yes, we can get into it. I know where Dad keeps all his keys and things. He doesn't know it, but I do. I can get the trunk open.'

'I won't ask you to do this,' Hefring said. There was a surprising gentleness to her voice that Ailsa hadn't ever heard there before. 'I cannot have you do anything you don't want to do. It has to be . . . your choice . . .'

She tried to say more, but all that came out was a dry, hacking cough. Her chest convulsed and she bent over, weak and in pain. Camilla reached out and put her arm around Hefring's shoulders as Ailsa put the tin mug back to her lips. Hefring let the water trickle into her mouth.

'Why now?' Ailsa asked. 'You've been under that cave for so long. You wanted us to leave you to die. We had to drag you every step of the way, like you didn't want any part in the world. Why do you want us to do this, now?'

Hefring closed her eyes before speaking.

'I was done, I had accepted my lot,' she whispered. 'I didn't want to die, but I didn't have the strength or the will to do much else. I didn't dare hope for anything else. My heart was sick. I was finished. Depressed, forgotten, left to rot and ready to do so.

'But then you came, child. You woke me up to the world. You showed me what it was to be young and free, to be wild, to be wilful. You reminded me of who I used to be. You showed me another way . . . you showed me that it was possible to hope again . . .

'You set me free,' she finished. 'First, you freed me from my cave. Then you set my mind free, reminded me of my old strength. Now, with just a little more help, I might be truly free . . .'

Ailsa nodded. She had seen it all. It reminded her of how her mum could be, how she had been when she was ill before. She would remember her strength, she would begin to fight, the sickness would lift, and she would become wilful and free once more.

'Aye, well then. We'll do it,' she said. 'We'll make you whole again. We'll help you to be free, won't we, Camilla?'

'Yes,' Camilla said firmly. Her eyes were fixed. There were no tears in them anymore.

Moxie panted, then barked, then howled aloud.

Twenty

Uncle Nod took Ailsa to visit her mum again the following morning. Her mum lay in a daze, sometimes muttering to herself, sometimes silent, only once seeming to realise that Ailsa was there at all.

'Love . . . love?' she asked.

'Aye, Mum, I'm here,' Ailsa replied, but it was too late. Her mum had drifted away again.

Ailsa tried to listen for her song, but it was hopeless, she thought. It seemed as though her mum's spirit had gone silent.

She took her mum's hand. 'Mum,' she whispered. 'Mum.'

Her mum's eyelids fluttered briefly, though she didn't wake. She slept on, comatose and uncaring.

Ailsa closed her eyes. She imagined the sea. She

pictured the waves churning and she tried to smell the salt spray and she tried to hear the howling wind and the sound of the water crashing against the rocks. She tried to hear Hefring's song, her rich, deep voice playing a melody below and above and throughout everything. She tried to remember how impossibly old the Earth felt as it answered Hefring's call, and she tried to remember how young and strong it could also feel.

Nothing much came to her. The hospital squashed it all. The bright corridor carried no songs. The ward was silent save for the buzz and hum of a few electronic monitors. It smelled of antiseptic.

It squashes it all, she thought, and she held her mum's hand tight.

'But you've got to try,' she whispered. 'You've got to listen for the song.'

Nothing happened. A light drizzle continued to patter against the ward's small window. The machines continued to hum. Her mum slept on, oblivious.

'Come home, Mum,' she whispered. 'I'll teach you the song. But you have to listen.'

*

She took Moxie out when she got back home, wandering through the drizzling rain. She buzzed at Camilla's, pressing the intercom button on the Galach house's gates.

'I'll be out in a second,' Camilla said breathlessly, before running out in her cagoule and boots.

They wandered down to the docks. The fishermen were done for the day and the docks and surrounding beaches were all empty.

'My dad says their days are numbered,' Camilla remarked as they walked along. 'He says there are hardly any fish left any more.'

'Aye?'

'Yes,' she said. 'Apparently we fish too much. The oceans are growing empty. Only trawlers like his that can go far out to sea are efficient anymore.'

Ailsa found a piece of driftwood and they began to throw it for Moxie. He leaped around, chasing after it, dropping it, playing with it and bringing it back with his head and tail held high for them to throw it again.

Camilla paused and took a deep breath as they both stood still. The rain thrummed against Ailsa's hood. It made Moxie's fur glisten. Camilla looked out to sea.

'I don't know if I can do it,' she said.

Ailsa was about to reply, but Camilla put a hand up to stop her.

'I know,' she snapped. Then she softened. 'I know I should do it. I think. But he's my daddy,' she said. 'I don't know if I can steal from him.'

She agonised over it for the rest of their walk.

'I'm frightened,' she admitted as they headed further along the coast. 'I know I have to do it. I must, so I will . . . I think I will. Yes, I will . . . but I'm still scared.'

'Aye,' Ailsa said. 'Of course you are. I am, too, to be honest. But we can't leave Hefring like she is. She's incomplete,' she carried on, thinking of her mum. 'Like a piece of her spirit is missing.'

'I know,' Camilla said. 'But I'm not just scared about getting caught. I'm scared about doing the right thing. I don't know what the right thing is . . . he's my daddy. It's my family.'

'Aye,' Ailsa nodded. 'Aye.'

Camilla flip-flopped. She changed her mind and then changed it back so many times that Ailsa lost count.

'I can do it,' she said, and then, immediately, 'I

don't think I can. I can't, I can't do it . . . I *shouldn't* do it . . .'

They came to the end of a wide bay. The sea's salt spray and the rain above pattered over them. Parts of the bay were cordoned off and newly fallen rocks lay scattered about. They turned back to head towards home and Camilla sagged. She looked defeated, as though she had argued herself to exhaustion. Ailsa turned to her and pulled her in, holding her tight.

Camilla took a deep breath.

'It's not my daddy's to keep,' she said. She closed her eyes. 'It's not my family's.'

Her voice was surprisingly firm. Ailsa let her go as her shoulders stiffened. Camilla took a step back and nodded.

'We won't miss it, surely,' she said, 'and it is Hefring's, after all. As you said, it's a part of her. She is incomplete.'

'Aye,' Ailsa agreed. 'But I know it's hard, all the same.'

'Yes, it is,' Camilla agreed.

They walked along in silence for a few minutes, crunching the wet sand and shingle beneath their boots. Moxie ran through the surf's shallows, splashing and prancing around.

'When will we do it?' Ailsa finally asked.

'We?' Camilla asked, surprised.

'Aye, of course,' Ailsa said. 'If you want. We'll find it together.'

'We'll steal it, you mean.'

'Steal it back,' Ailsa insisted.

'Yes,' Camilla conceded. 'I would like that, though. Both of us together.'

'Aye, so when?' Ailsa asked.

'Tomorrow,' Camilla said.

'Aye?'

Camilla nodded. 'Yes,' she said. 'My family have been invited to an evening thing, somewhere on the mainland. A gala of some sort. I'll pretend I'm ill and they'll go without me.'

'Will that work?'

Camilla shrugged. 'I've done it before,' she said. 'They don't really care, to be honest.'

'Do we need to prepare anything?' Ailsa asked.

'No, I shouldn't think so,' Camilla said. 'I'll open the back gate for you. It's easy to find. Daddy's men only watch the front.'

'Aye.'

'I'll sneak into his office,' Camilla continued. 'I know where he keeps his keys. I had a chance to look this morning and there are a few that I think it could be. I'll have them ready, then we can go up to the loft. You can take the sea-skin home, then we'll take it to Hefring when we can.'

'Aye,' Ailsa said. She frowned. 'He might notice it at some point, though,' she said. 'Your parents will probably know it was us.'

'They never go up there, but yes, they will find out some day,' Camilla said. 'But it's the right thing to do, isn't it? And anyway, I go back to school in a few weeks, so I'll be away from Daddy and his temper. I'll be long gone before he realises anything's amiss.'

Twenty-one

The Galachs went out for the evening as planned. Camilla feigned illness and they left her behind. Ailsa watched the Galachs' car pull out of the drive and then, ten minutes later, she sneaked over to the house. There was a car parked across the street from their gates. The usual men were sitting inside, gazing into the darkness. Ailsa went around to a small side gate towards the back of the house, near where the walls met the sheer cliff drop. Camilla had left it open for her and she slipped in.

Camilla was waiting by the house's side door to usher her in.

'So far, so good,' Camilla said. She tried to smile but Ailsa could see that she was nervous.

'Aye, it's going to be OK,' Ailsa told her.

Camilla nodded and breathed deeply. She held out her hand. There was a bunch of old, small keys on it. 'I took them from Daddy's office a couple of hours ago,' she said. 'They're the only ones for which I don't know a use, and they look right, don't they?'

Ailsa nodded. Some of them looked very much like they belonged to old fashioned, chunky padlocks.

'Aye, I reckon so,' she said.

They went up into the loft. Camilla pulled the ladder down once more, climbed up and pushed the hatch open. She turned the lights on as Ailsa climbed up, poking her head into the loft.

Camilla was already halfway across the room by the time Ailsa pulled herself up. Dust swirled around her feet. It was as thick as she remembered, laying in a dense coat over all the old boxes and disused furniture.

She followed Camilla over to the trunks in the far corner, where she was sorting through the keys, holding each one up to the main padlock on the dusty, large trunk.

If anything, the trunk looked sturdier now than it had before. It was stubborn and strong, Ailsa thought. The iron bands around its edges and corners held fast. The two padlocks holding it closed sat heavy and still.

Camilla found a likely looking key from the ring. It was a large bronze one that seemed to be the right size for both locks.

'This one, I think,' she muttered to herself. She tried it in the first padlock. It went in, but wouldn't turn, and she cursed under her breath.

'Try the other lock,' Ailsa said, but Camilla was already moving to do so.

This time, the key went in and turned a little. 'It's rusted shut . . .' Camilla said. 'I don't know if I can open it . . .'

'Come here,' Ailsa said.

Camilla shifted over and let Ailsa have a go. She tried to turn the key. It wiggled around a little, but the mechanism was stiff. Red, rusty flakes seeped from inside the lock. Ailsa felt herself go red. She held her breath and turned, putting all her strength into it.

Finally, with a satisfying click and another trickle of rust, the key turned.

'Ah,' Ailsa gasped, letting it go.

She massaged her fingers and hand, stiff from pushing

so hard, a little bruised against the key. As she did so, Camilla pulled the padlock off and started searching through the keys once more.

'That one,' Ailsa said, spotting a likely looking one.

It was long and black, made from iron, the same as the padlock. Camilla put it into the lock and turned it. It stuck again, but she grunted, and the lock sprang open. She pulled it off the trunk and threw the lid open.

The inside of the trunk was cavernous and nearly empty. It was all hard wood and dust. And just there, at the back, in a corner, in the gloom, was a little parcel. It was wrapped in dull coloured, waxy cloth.

'Oilcloth, like you get on a sou'wester,' Ailsa said. 'Uncle Nod's always got stuff like this lying about.'

It was tied with old fishing line, tightly knotted. Camilla lifted it out and eyed it closely.

'Do you think this is it?' she asked.

'Let's see,' Ailsa said. She took up the keyring, found a particularly jagged toothed key, and sawed through the fishing line. It was tough. It took some getting through. It pinged apart in the end, however, splitting as the key's teeth cut through it.

Ailsa sat down, cross legged, and unwrapped it, letting the oilcloth unfold on her lap.

They both gasped.

It was incredibly fine, like silk. Ailsa turned the oilcloth over and the sea-skin poured out into her hand. Camilla reached out to touch it and sighed. The skin shimmered, almost see-through, as Ailsa held it up to the light. Fine scales coated one side of it. They seemed to ripple in the light. They were a soft grey at first, then turquoise, then a subtle violet, then a blue so pale they were almost white.

'It's beautiful,' Ailsa whispered.

'It's impossible,' Camilla replied.

The sound of tyres crunching on gravel grew loud outside.

Camilla swore.

'It's my parents!' she said. She hastily closed the trunk and put the locks back on. There were smears all over it where they had both rubbed the dust off, and she blurred them out with the edge of her sleeve as Ailsa wrapped the sea-skin back up in the oilcloth.

'Come on!' Camilla hissed.

She grabbed Ailsa's arm and they both ran back to the

ladder, slapping the light switch off as they went. Ailsa dropped the sea-skin, but Camilla stooped, picked it up and stuffed it up her jumper. They both slid down the ladder, closing the hatch behind them and then pushing it up and away.

'Come here,' Ailsa said.

Camilla was covered in dust. She wiped as much of it off as possible, then Camilla did the same for her.

They ran down the landing and made it to the stairs as the front door opened.

Camilla's parents were arguing. Suzanne slunk in behind them, came upstairs, and rolled her eyes at Camilla as she passed them. She stomped her feet as she got to the landing.

Mrs Galach was unsteady on her feet. She cursed. Spittle flecked her chin. Mr Galach was red-faced. He kept cracking his knuckles and a steady stream of whispered swear words hissed from between his clenched lips.

They stopped arguing when they saw Camilla and Ailsa on the stairs. Mrs Galach frowned at them.

'I thought you were sick,' she said to Camilla.

'I am,' Camilla replied. 'Ailsa just popped in to see how I was doing. She's going now, though. I'll see her out.'

They both hurried downstairs and pushed past Camilla's parents as Mr Galach swore once more and stomped away, echoing Suzanne, and muttered something about needing a whisky.

Camilla and Ailsa headed out the door and into the garden. Dusk was swallowing the world and the rain was coming down hard. When they were away from the house's lights, Camilla pulled out the oilcloth and thrust it into Ailsa's hands.

'Keep it safe tonight,' she said.

'Will you be OK?' Ailsa asked.

Camilla nodded. She was shaking. 'I should be able to sneak Daddy's keys back into his office later on, when they're all in bed,' she said.

'Aye, then,' Ailsa said. 'I'll see you tomorrow.'

'Meet me at the end of the road.'

'Aye.'

Ailsa nodded. She stuffed the oilcloth up her own shirt. It was cold and soft against her skin. Then she noticed Camilla's eyes. They were wide, as ever, and they seemed to shimmer despite the evening's twilit darkness. They shone with a couple of tears. Her cheeks were pale and flushed and her lips were red.

'Tomorrow,' Camilla said.

'Aye,' Ailsa choked.

'This will all be worth it.'

'Aye.'

Ailsa hurried home through the gathering darkness and the downpour. Her heart hammered and her breath was short.

Moxie barked at the door as she ran up the garden path, splashing through puddles. He leaped up onto his hind legs as she pushed it open. Wagging, whining with joy, he placed his forepaws on her shoulders and licked her face. His breath was hot, and she clung to him.

'Hello, love,' Uncle Nod said. He was pacing nervously around the kitchen.

Aunt Bertha was at the table. Where Uncle Nod looked anxious, she looked serene.

'You been at the Galachs, seeing that young Camilla?' Uncle Nod asked. His voice broke slightly.

Ailsa nodded.

'Good, that's good,' he muttered. 'Good friends are always . . . good.'

'Oh, for goodness' sake, Nod!' Aunt Bertha snapped. 'Will you calm down and stop babbling?'

'Aye,' Uncle Nod replied. 'Aye, well. Yes. Aye.'

'What's wrong?' Ailsa asked, impatient. 'What's happened?'

Aunt Bertha took a deep breath. 'Your mum's upstairs,' she said. Her voice was level. 'The doctors said they couldn't do much more for her, but that she was stable for the moment. She wanted to come home.'

'And your aunt agreed to it—' Uncle Nod began.

'We *both* agreed to it,' Aunt Bertha said firmly. She looked at Ailsa. 'She's asleep upstairs. You can go in to see her, but be quiet, hen. She needs her rest.'

'Aye, Aunt Bertha,' Ailsa replied. Her eyes stung. The oilcloth seemed warm beneath her top as she went upstairs.

Ailsa went into her mum's bedroom. She was hopeful. It was surely a good sign that they had let her come home, wasn't it?

She looked down at her mum. She looked half-dead,

like she was hardly breathing. Her skin was cold and waxen and there were great rings under her eyes. There was nothing good that she could see, but at least her mum was away from that awful hospital.

Ailsa opened the window. The rain danced around outside, cooling the air so that a cold breeze blew. It was needed, Ailsa thought. Hefring would sing her song again.

'And you need to listen out for it, Mum,' she whispered, coming back to her mum's bed. 'Please, please listen for it. Wake up and hear it. You have to. It's life. It's sadness, but it's joy, too . . . There is so much in it. It's . . . it's everything we're missing here, everything you're missing.

'Mum, Mum,' she whispered urgently. 'Mum, I found a strange woman in a cave.' She forced herself to say it, screwing up every ounce of willpower she had. 'I was scared and I didn't know what to do. I'm not scared, now. I know what to do . . . I'm doing it. I'm helping her. I'm helping her like I can't help you, but like I wish I could . . .'

Her mum carried on lying there, still as a statue, undisturbed as a cool breeze blew, ruffling the curtains ever so slightly.

Twenty-two

Camilla and Ailsa met up the following day, as planned. Camilla looked as though she had hardly slept. She was pale and there were dark rings under her eyes. Ailsa had only managed a couple of hours of sleep herself, so she suspected that she looked much the same. Only Moxie seemed spry, excited to be going back over to the lighthouse once more.

The lighthouse's front door was darkened with damp. The moss coating the front steps leading up to it had grown thicker and the smell of brine was overpowering. It was like the whole lighthouse was beginning to rot.

It got worse inside.

'Oh, my,' Camilla gasped.

Ailsa wrinkled her nose. Puddles lay all about, warping

the floorboards. Thick barnacles clung to the bannisters and the stalactites overhead had grown longer and sharper. They dripped cold water onto Ailsa and Camilla's heads as they made their way upstairs to Hefring.

They found Hefring slumped in the middle of the room, barely conscious. Dead, half eaten things lay all around her. Chocolate wrappers were mixed in with the dead things, and blood and chocolate stained Hefring's mouth and chin. The smell made them both gag. Moxie's nose went wild, twitching, and he backed away to the edge of the room.

'Is . . . is she still breathing?' Camilla asked.

Hefring grunted. 'I'm not dead yet . . . little *dronning . . .*' she whispered. Her voice was hoarse yet gentle, like a soft breeze blowing through bare, winter's trees.

'Did . . . did you bring it?' she asked. She could barely lift her head to look at them. 'I feel it . . . I feel it . . .'

'Aye,' Ailsa said. She dropped her rucksack from her back, crouched down and unzipped it. The oilcloth was folded inside. She brought it out and carefully unfolded it all. The sea-skin was as beautiful as before, its silvered scales soft to the touch.

The change was sudden.

Hefring swore. She gasped. Her head came up fast. Outside, the wind roared and keened. The sea churned, buffeting the rocks with everything it had as Hefring gazed at Ailsa. Those beautiful, sad eyes welled up as Ailsa met them with her own. Her own heart beat hard in her chest as the gale threatened to smash through the balcony doors. She could have sworn she felt the lighthouse swaying before such a bad storm.

Then it quietened. Ailsa wasn't even sure it had been there.

The smell of rotten flesh diminished. It had been enough to draw tears to Ailsa and Camilla's eyes, but the air sweetened as Ailsa unveiled the sea-skin. The smell disappeared, swept away as though blown by a fresh breeze. Springtime smells seemed to replace it, sun-dried sand and the warm throb of nature, the harmony of new life.

Hefring herself began to change too, right in front of them. Her sad, beautiful eyes had always been sunk deep into folds of hooded, leathery skin. However, the skin began to smooth. The hoods withdrew and her eyes gleamed, looking suddenly young and bright. The lines across her face began to smooth too, like they were being rubbed out, like the clock was being turned backwards. Her thin, bitter lips filled out. As Ailsa watched, they turned plump. They framed a wide, dazzling smile as all around seemed to grow light.

It wasn't just Hefring's face, either. Her limp, lank hair brightened, almost glowing golden blonde. It grew lustrous and wavy, and began to flow around her, over her shoulders.

Though her movements were stiff and laboured as she climbed to her feet, she managed to stand straight, with her chin raised and her shoulders back. Her scrawny arms and weak, scarred legs filled out. New muscle seemed to swell until she was suddenly clean limbed and strong. The ravaged skin all over her body healed up. Sores and bruises faded, lesions and cuts closed, rough skin smoothed. Sagging flesh became tight, pale and healthy, as though it could barely contain the power within her any more.

Hefring had her eyes fixed on Ailsa and the sea-skin throughout. She grew taller as she changed. Her strength radiated from her, almost dizzying as the two girls watched.

Even the room began to change. Though nothing looked too different, the feeling of rot and decay faded quickly. It was replaced by verdancy, bursting with new life. Hefring herself was warm and full of life. Her skin and the room around her seemed to glow faintly, as though the light of the moon and the sun and the stars bathed her.

Anything felt possible bathed in Hefring's brightness. Everything felt possible and beautiful and light.

Hefring came to stand before Ailsa and reached out a hand for her sea-skin, smiling all the while as though dazed, as though dreaming. Ailsa noticed that her clawed talons were no more. They had been replaced by five elegant fingers on each hand, smooth and subtle.

Within a few short moments, she had turned from the haggard, corpse-like ghoul they had first known, into a young looking, vibrant woman, full of the power of life. Clear eyes met Ailsa's as Hefring took the sea-skin. Tears streamed down her perfect cheeks. She smiled. Ailsa saw that her teeth were still like needles, still sharp and pointed, though they had turned pearly white and clear.

Hefring hugged the sea-skin to her breast. She buried her face in it like a child with their comfort blanket. Great wracking sobs heaved through her body for a moment, desperate and tragic and hopeful all at once. They came, they shook, and then Hefring began to grow still. She breathed deeply and looked up at Ailsa and Camilla.

'You wonderful girls,' she said quietly, lowering her sea-skin. Her words were honeyed and warm. They filled Ailsa's heart.

'Thank you,' Hefring said. 'Thank you.'

Joy eddied through the room. It focussed around Hefring, almost intoxicating. The aching sadness was gone, banished as her whole being seemed to fill and burst with the thrill of life.

Then Hefring folded her sea-skin over one arm. She smiled and gestured for them to follow her. Moxie gladly trotted along at her side. Ailsa let Camilla go first, then followed along. They left the room and headed downstairs. Flowers had replaced the mould, growing through cracks in the walls. Yellow sand and rich, silty earth lay in patches on the floor where the puddles and damp had been.

It was like something had woken up, Ailsa thought. It felt like the world around her was getting better.

They carried on outside, into the falling rain, crossing the finger of rock in a procession, Hefring, Moxie, Camilla, then finally Ailsa. Hefring led them down onto the beach, where Ailsa and Camilla had spent a blisteringly hot day playing in the sun what felt like an age ago.

'*Mine venner*,' Hefring said, turning to them. 'My friends, my wonderful friends. You restored me. Listen for my song, my loves. It will always play for you. This is my promise.'

She stooped down and kissed them each on the cheek. Her lips were soft, and her skin smelled fresh and wild. She kneeled in the sand, stroked Moxie, and laughed.

'*Glodhund*, oh *glodhund*,' she crooned to him. 'Keep them well,' she told him, and kissed the top of his head.

Then she stood and turned, facing out to the sea.

The song came much as it had done before. Hefring closed her eyes, lifting her face to the heavens. The drizzle shimmered around her as a halo.

However, where before she had been a performer, singing her song to the world, now she was more like the conductor of a chorus. The ground beneath their feet felt

227

alive. It didn't move. Nothing so obvious happened. But Ailsa felt it beckon to them, as though the whole world were turning for this moment. The air grew cold. It danced on her skin. The wind howled, churning the clouds above, beating the clifftops behind them, pulling at their hair.

Then the music came. This time, the world didn't seem to hold its breath. It sang for Hefring, jubilant and joyful. It was something felt as much as heard. Deep melodies spoke of hardship and heartbreak. High notes danced above it all, happy and excited. Every range, every emotion, every thought and feeling ever thought or felt. It played through the earth and the sky, the sea and the wind. It played through the four of them, reverberating from and around and within Hefring.

It shimmered and it danced once more, almost visible in its liveliness.

The sea rose, foaming, climbing a few metres up the beach. It crashed against the rocks and the sand. For a second, Ailsa thought she saw shapes in its surf. They were like children, running and dancing through the water, made of the water, eyes glowing softly as they watched her, and then they were gone.

Finally, Hefring added her own voice to the song.

What came out was clear and beautiful. It made Ailsa think of mountain streams, frozen and pure. It was angry too, ferocious, like thundering waterfalls and giant waves pulling ships to the deeps. At times it grew ugly, even, and Hefring once more began to resemble the strange woman she had been when Ailsa first found her. But it came back. Hefring grew beautiful again in turn. Her song was all things. Rage and peace were held in its notes, as were joy and sadness, order and madness, and everything in between. All was within her grasp.

It was Hefring's song, and it was the song of the sea.

Then it dimmed down, then it ended. Hefring sighed and the music ceased.

Ailsa's face was wet. She had no idea where her tears ended and the rainwater began.

Moxie whimpered and flicked his tail, satisfied with it all.

Hefring didn't say another word. She simply walked towards the water as Ailsa watched. As the first shallow surf washed over her toes, she threw her sea-skin around her shoulders. It clung to her body like gauze, like a silken robe. Then a large wave rose before her. Ailsa saw bright lights flickering inside, blinking, watching. Whatever they were, they had come for Hefring.

The wave swelled above Hefring, swept over her, and she was gone.

The winds began to howl once more as Ailsa and Camilla walked home together. The sea began to rise. Neither girl said too much to the other. They didn't really need to.

Twenty-three

There was a great storm that night. The rain hammered harder than ever at Ailsa's bedroom window. It seemed to hammer the whole coast. Gale force winds crashed against the house, shaking the walls, as stray bins and scrap flew about all around outside. Ailsa could just about hear the roaring waves pummelling the rocks along the shore beneath it all. She knelt on her bed with her nose pressed to the windowpane, watching through the inky blackness as the storm washed over everything.

Moxie slunk into Ailsa's room and leaped up onto her bed beside her. She was scared, and she welcomed him as he curled up against her. His nearness gave her comfort as a great booming thunderclap rocked the skies.

Sirens blazed a couple of times. Flashing blue lights

cut through the darkness and the rain, though the world outside was too distorted for her to properly see where they were coming from. The ground itself seemed to shake a few times.

Uncle Nod came in to check on her at one point.

'You OK, love?' he asked.

'Aye,' she said.

He came to sit on the side of her bed and put his great arms around her and Moxie.

'This daft wee beggar will look after you,' he said, scratching Moxie behind the ears. 'He's braver and tougher than he looks.'

'Aye,' she said. She smiled at her uncle, then frowned. 'There were sirens,' she said.

'Aye,' Uncle Nod said. 'There's been some more subsidence. Not surprising, in all of this. Some of the coast is coming apart, though when I went out for a look, they told me to stay in. Batten down the hatches till it passes, and all that.'

'Aye.'

Uncle Nod left her to sleep, but soon enough a familiar feeling crept over her. Hefring's song came to her through the storm. The roar of the waves, the wind and the rain stayed the same. But Hefring's power was there. It was everywhere, filled with anger and joy, filled with something primal.

'Come on, boy,' she whispered to Moxie.

They both padded silently through to her mum's room.

The whole house shook, but this was far too important. She closed the door and opened her mum's window. A great, wet wind buffeted in straight away, howling into the room.

'Listen, Mum,' Ailsa said. 'It's the song. It's Hefring's song. It's the world's song. You need to listen, Mum. We all need to add our own songs to it. It's the only way to live . . . to feel alive.'

She climbed into bed next to her mum. She pulled the covers close and cuddled in, one arm around her mum's chest. Moxie curled up on the floor. Despite the roar and the thunder outside, she slept peacefully for the first time in a long time. She didn't stir all night, nor did she dream.

The sun was high in the sky when she opened her eyes the following morning. Its light filtered in through the crack in her mum's curtains, dazzlingly bright. The air was clear and crisp. Her mum was completely still next to her, though she seemed a little warmer than she had been.

Perhaps it's just wishful thinking, Ailsa told herself. But she wasn't sure. Her mum had a little colour in her cheeks.

'The world's remembered that it's supposed to be summer,' Uncle Nod said when Ailsa went down to the kitchen. The whole room was bathed in honey coloured sunshine. Outside, the skies were bright blue.

'Aye, and about time, too,' Aunt Bertha said, coming in from the garden. A faint layer of sweat glistened on her forehead, though she was covered in mud nearly up to her knees. 'Last night it must have all blown itself out.'

Aunt Bertha sat at the table and Ailsa slid into a chair opposite her.

'You look fresher than you have in a while, hen,' Aunt Bertha said. 'Don't tell me you managed to sleep through all that racket last night?'

'Aye,' Ailsa said. 'I was scared, but still. I slept for hours and hours.' She shrugged.

'You're the only one who did,' Uncle Nod complained.

234

He brought a bowl, a spoon, a box of cereal and some milk over and set it all down in front of Ailsa.

'Aye?' Ailsa asked, helping herself to some breakfast.

'Aye,' Uncle Nod said. 'Half the harbour's been torn to pieces.'

'Oh no,' Ailsa said. 'Is everyone OK?'

Uncle Nod shrugged. 'Everyone's fine. Just most of the boats are wrecked. The boys are all happy, though, I think,' he told her. 'They weren't catching any fish anyway. At least now they'll be able to claim on insurance. They're all due a big payday soon enough, though I don't know what'll come next. Anyway, the Galachs fared worse.'

'What happened?'

'Their trawlers went down, for starters,' Uncle Nod told her. He sat down heavily next to Aunt Bertha. 'They bore the brunt of the damage. One went down completely and the other's half a wreck. It's worth more as scrap metal now than as a boat, I'd say.'

'Aye?'

'Aye,' Uncle Nod sighed. 'Of course, they'll get money off their insurance too, so there's that. But there'll be no local fish coming in any time soon.'

'Typical!' Aunt Bertha snapped.

'What?' Uncle Nod asked, looking shocked.

'Half the Galachs' house falls into the sea and all you can think about is the boats!'

'Aye, well,' Uncle Nod grumbled. He shrugged.

'What happened to their house?' Ailsa asked. Her heart started to pound. She dropped her spoon.

'I told you some of the cliffs took it bad,' Uncle Nod said. 'Well, the subsidence hit them worse than anyone.'

'Aye,' Aunt Bertha concurred. 'The fire brigade has been round. Don't worry,' she said, seeing the look on Ailsa's face. 'Nobody's hurt. But the cliffs at the end of their garden gave in, and they took the back of the house with them.'

'I've got to go and see Camilla,' Ailsa said. She was on her feet and hurrying out of the house before either her aunt or uncle could say a word.

There was a fire engine parked outside Camilla's house. A crowd stood around about, opposite the house, staring. A black car pulled out of the front gates as Ailsa hurried over. Mrs Galach was driving. As it passed by, Ailsa saw that Camilla and Suzanne were in the back. She tried to catch Camilla's eye, but Camilla seemed to be pointedly staring dead ahead as the crowd watched.

Ailsa saw the police van last. She joined the crowd of onlookers. She saw a few of the men she knew from the docks standing nearby. Mrs Tomlinson was near the back of the crowd, her arms crossed over her chest. Everyone was whispering to one another.

The house was crooked. Parts of the sides were crumbling. The back had fallen away completely, along with the cliffs' edges, just as Uncle Nod had said. The whole garden was cordoned off.

The whispering got worse when a couple of police officers came out of the Galachs' house. They were flanking Mr Galach. His hands were bound in handcuffs. He wore dark glasses that flashed in the bright sunshine, and he refused to look at the crowd as people began to take pictures.

Ailsa went over to Mrs Tomlinson. 'What's going on?' she asked.

'It seems the Galachs have finally been caught out,' Mrs Tomlinson replied.

'What?'

'Apparently the landslide broke Mr Galach's office in half. When the fire brigade got here, they saw a few things in there that Mr Galach wouldn't have wanted them to,' Mrs Tomlinson said.

'Things he shouldn't have. Criminal things, apparently,' a fisherman added, joining the conversation. 'They called the police. And apparently Mrs Galach's having none of it. She's packed the girls up and gone to her sister's place.'

'Aye, though we all knew he was a real gangster,' another fisherman said. He nodded towards the police officers bringing Mr Galach out. 'This is just the tip of the iceberg, by some reckonings.'

'Though you don't need to know the ins and outs,' Mrs Tomlinson told Ailsa, looking pointedly at the fishermen.

'Oh, aye,' the first one murmured. 'No, of course not. Aye.'

The police officers put Mr Galach in the back of the van and locked the doors. A third came over to the crowd, ushering them away so that they could bring the van through.

Ailsa had had enough. She had seen enough. The day was warm and bright, but her heart was heavy. She felt like she had a lead weight in her stomach. As the crowd continued to gawp, and as the van tried to pull away from the house, she trudged back up the road to her aunt and uncle's house.

However, as Ailsa pushed the kitchen door open, she came up short. Uncle Nod was in the corner, beaming. Aunt Bertha was at the sink, looking like she was torn between laughing and crying. Ailsa's mum was sitting at the kitchen table, nursing a cup of tea.

'Hello, love,' she said, as Ailsa came in.

Twenty-four

There wasn't much to her mum. She was bone thin. Every angle in her body looked sharp. Her collarbone was jutting out, her neck was tiny, like a little bird's, and her knuckles looked like stones bulging from her hands. Her skin was waxy, too, almost see-through and pasty, unhealthy looking. There were great, dark circles under her eyes, and her eyes themselves were yellowed and bloodshot.

Ailsa imagined that her mum almost had talons at the ends of her fingers. She imagined that she almost had sores and scales on her skin.

But her mum was smiling. She was smiling for the first time in weeks, maybe months. There was peace and happiness in her, around her. It floated like a breeze and filled the kitchen with a quiet kind of calm.

Her smile lit up her tired, yellowed eyes. Though they looked unwell, they sparkled. There was a great life to them. There was strength in them that it seemed her mum was remembering.

'I woke up feeling strong,' she told Ailsa. Her voice was quiet but firm. She rose from the kitchen table, pushing against it with those thin, hard hands, coming up tall.

'And with all the sunshine, well . . .'

She trailed off. Her smile wavered slightly as she looked at Ailsa, but Ailsa was past noticing. She was beyond anything but the moment. She launched herself across the room. It felt like her feet didn't even touch the ground, as though she were flying. Her mum caught her, and they clung to one another.

'Mummy, my mummy,' Ailsa whispered as she buried her head in her mum's hair.

Her mum still smelled of her mum. It wasn't the musty smell of a bedridden patient. It wasn't the smell of dead things, the dockyard stench Ailsa had come to expect from anybody in pain. It was warmth, a human smell, a lively scent that she had known since her earliest memories.

'My mum,' she whispered again, feeling like a small, small child. She felt at home for the first time in months.

'Aye, love,' her mum whispered back. She held Ailsa tight and kissed her and kept kissing her.

Aunt Bertha joined them at some point. Uncle Nod came, too. They all stood huddled together, arms around one another, with Ailsa in the middle of it all. She cried. Her mum cried, Uncle Nod cried, and Aunt Bertha chuckled and shook as she pulled them all in together.

Then they stepped apart and Ailsa's mum looked down at her. She smiled and she nodded. She looked at Uncle Nod and Aunt Bertha.

'Look at my girl, my beautiful girl,' she said. 'Thank you, thank you so much for taking care of her.'

'Aw, don't be daft,' Uncle Nod said. Then he started crying again and Ailsa, her mum and Aunt Bertha all began to laugh.

'Ah, what a foolish sight we all make,' Aunt Bertha said.

'Come on, love, let's go outside and get some air,' Aunt Bertha said to Ailsa's mum a little later on.

Ailsa made some tea. She boiled the kettle and found the teabags, throwing them into four big, chipped mugs. As the kettle wobbled and whistled away, she put a lump of sugar into her own mug, and one into her mum's, just the way they both liked it.

'Biscuits too, I'd say,' Uncle Nod said.

'Aye,' Ailsa agreed. She looked at her mum, thin and wiry, and reached for the biscuit tin, plonking it down on the countertop.

'You three head out, now,' Uncle Nod said. 'I've got a couple of phone calls to make. I'll be out in a bit.'

'Who are you calling, Uncle Nod?' Ailsa asked.

'The good doctor, for one.'

'Dr Arbuthnot?'

'Aye, he'll want to know all about everything.'

'I should say,' Ailsa's mum said. 'I've never . . . you know . . . rallied this quick.'

They all took their cups of tea and the three of them headed out into the garden whilst Uncle Nod stayed inside. There was a table and chairs in the corner of the yard, with a big parasol standing proud over them. Birds skimmed overhead, loud gulls cawing, and a couple of seabirds Ailsa didn't recognise. Somewhere nearby, a songbird tooted merrily to the day.

Her mum sat down and sighed. She closed her eyes, leaned back in her chair, breathed deeply, and smiled.

'It feels good to be out,' she said. 'Part of the world again.'

Uncle Nod got through to Dr Arbuthnot's office as they sat in the sunshine, drinking their tea. Dr Arbuthnot came round a few hours later, just after lunch. His car pulled up, grumbling and rumbling in the street, and his hurried footsteps clacked against the garden path.

He was shocked when he saw Ailsa's mum.

'This is incredible,' he muttered to himself.

He and Ailsa's mum went off alone into her room for a long time. There was laughter at one point, which shocked Ailsa. They both looked satisfied when they came out again. Everyone gathered in the kitchen, standing in the sunshine as it cascaded in through the open window.

'Incredible, incredible,' Dr Arbuthnot said, shaking his head. 'It's remarkable progress indeed. Of course, it's early days. Very early days.'

He looked at Ailsa's mum and nodded to himself.

'But incredible nonetheless,' he said. 'I'll see you again the day after tomorrow. Keep an eye on things, close tabs, and all that. But we can talk about bringing some of your medicines down soon enough. Get you feeling yourself again.'

'Absolutely,' Ailsa's mum replied. 'Myself again.'

'Now, go, get yourselves out,' Dr Arbuthnot said, gesturing to the kitchen window. 'Go and enjoy this wonderful weather.'

They did exactly that, heading out once more. Ailsa's mum wanted to spend every minute she could out in the garden. They sat in the shade for the whole of the rest of the day, lounging by the garden table beneath the parasol. Her mum's skin was so pale it was almost see-through, and any sunlight would burn her worse than Ailsa's own burns had been. But, in the cool, with the sun dazzling all around them, her mum reacquainted herself with the world.

'It's so beautiful,' she sighed at one point. 'You almost forget . . . it's so easy to.'

'Aye,' Ailsa said. She sat huddled close to her mum. She felt clingy, like a small child, though she didn't make any effort to stop. Her mum let her. She welcomed it. They both clung to one another, and, in those small, warm moments, Ailsa felt peace for the first time in a long time.

She wondered about Hefring. She wondered where she was, what she was doing.

'Penny for your thoughts,' her mum said at one point.

'I'm just remembering a friend,' Ailsa replied. 'And a song she once taught me.'

'Funny you say that,' her mum said. 'I had the strangest dream last night.'

'Aye?'

'There was an amazing song in it, though it wasn't quite a song . . .' her mum said. 'I don't really know how to describe it.'

'Like it was everything that's ever been, a feeling as much as a sound, like the whole world's singing it out,' Ailsa said.

Her mum looked at her strangely.

'Aye, exactly like that, love,' she said. 'And it was like the world was somehow lighter for letting out its song. Like I was lighter for hearing it. I felt like an old friend was teaching me it, though for the life of me I couldn't say who it was.'

Ailsa nodded. 'Aye,' she said.

'Then I woke up feeling . . . well, just better,' her mum finished.

Ailsa thought about telling her mum about Hefring. She nearly did. Then, as she was about to begin, about to form the words, she changed her mind. Thinking about it, she realised she didn't really want to, after all. Her mum had heard the song. Not much else mattered beyond that.

Twenty-five

The following day dawned as warm, bright and clear as the previous one. Birds sang in the yard, the distant sound of the docks clamoured in the air as people began to clear the wreckage, and the air hummed with honeyed sunlight.

As Ailsa got out of bed, she heard rustling and movement from her mum's room. She crept along the hallway and peeked inside through the half open door. Moxie was there, jumping about, excited. Her mum was stripping the sheets from her bed, throwing them into a pile to be washed. A stack of clean bedding sat on a chest of drawers, ready to be used.

The room was still dark, though. It still felt dingy to Ailsa.

'Want a hand, Mum?' she asked.

'Aye, love, that'd be great,' her mum replied, smiling. She was red faced. The exertion of stripping her bed was almost too much. But she looked happy, still.

'Did you sleep OK?' her mum began, but she fell quiet as Ailsa strode over to the window.

The windows themselves were shut tight and the curtains were drawn over them.

That won't do, Ailsa thought to herself.

She ripped the curtains apart, letting the dazzling summer light spill in. It chased shadows around the room, chewing them up, as she tied the curtains into place. The gloom evaporated all at once. Moxie danced in the sunshine, yipping excitedly to himself.

Next, she threw the windows open. A sweet summer breeze floated in, stirring up motes of dust, blowing through the stale air. It ruffled Moxie's fur. Gulls cawed in the background.

That's how it should be, Ailsa thought.

She turned to face her mum. Her mum had her eyes closed and she was breathing deeply, a look of bliss on her face.

'Aye, that's better,' her mum said, opening her eyes once more. She squinted a little still through the light, more accustomed to being in darkness, but she stood firm before it.

Ailsa grabbed a pillow and pulled the cover off it, throwing it into the pile along with the rest of the old bedding.

They ate their breakfast at the kitchen table, munching on toast and sipping strong, sweet tea. Aunt Bertha came in from the garden, fetched herself a cup and sat with them. Uncle Nod came in after a little while, yawning widely and stretching his arms out to the sides. A couple of pops sounded, his joints loosening for the day.

'Aye, well,' he said sluggishly. He grinned around the kitchen. Then he noticed the sunshine streaming in.

'It's too nice a day to be around the house,' he said. 'And we've not much work on for the moment. Not till they salvage what can be salvaged down at the docks. There's a great spot for a picnic not far off, if anyone's up for it?'

'Yes please!' Ailsa said before anyone else could speak.

She couldn't think of anything she would rather do than spend another day in the sunshine with Mum, Uncle Nod, Aunt Bertha and Moxie. The world had woken up, it seemed, and she was as eager as ever to get out into it.

'Aye, well then,' Uncle Nod said. 'I'll put some bits together.'

He and Ailsa made some sandwiches, cutting cheese and slices of ham, layering them in the bread with butter and pickle. Uncle Nod packed them in a rucksack with some cans of fizzy drink and a flask of tea. Ailsa added the last of Mrs Tomlinson's chocolate cake and a bag of treats for Moxie, who sniffed around them both the whole time, begging for scraps.

'You daft old thing,' Uncle Nod chuckled. Then, when he thought no one was looking, he threw Moxie a couple of treats.

Ailsa smiled to herself, pretending not to have seen.

Both daft old things, she thought to herself.

They left mid-morning, planning to drive up to Uncle Nod's spot, planning to spend as much of the day as possible out beneath the wide, blue sky and clear, bright sun. Sunshine beat down all around them.

251

Ailsa made sure that her mum put on plenty of sun cream. 'We can't have you burning,' she said as she handed Mum the bottle.

Uncle Nod and Aunt Bertha shared a look. Ailsa caught them and blushed.

'Aye, well,' she said.

'Aye, you're not wrong, love,' Aunt Bertha said kindly.

'And there's no better teacher than experience, is there?' Uncle Nod asked, hefting the picnic basket under one arm, and leading the way out to the car.

Ailsa and Moxie jumped into the back of the car. It was hot and sticky from sitting in the sunshine and Moxie began to pant, though Ailsa rolled down both the windows before putting her seatbelt on. Mum was about to get in, but she stopped. She looked up as Uncle Nod and Aunt Bertha finished loading the car. She squinted into the sunlight.

'Who's that, then?' she asked. 'Sitting on the wall, there.'

'Blimey,' Uncle Nod said. 'It's Camilla Galach.'

Ailsa whirled around in her seat, nearly strangling herself on her seatbelt. Moxie sat bolt upright and began to whine and wag his tail. Ailsa clambered out awkwardly and Moxie bounded out behind her.

Camilla was sitting on a low wall a little way along the road. Her cheeks were red, and her eyes looked puffy. A bicycle was propped up next to her. She saw them watching her and got up from the wall. She couldn't meet their gaze. She thrust her hands into her pockets, blushed and stared pointedly above Ailsa's head. Then she stared down at her feet, kicking at the dusty road.

Ailsa thought she looked awful. She looked like she hadn't slept in days, like she had spent hours and hours crying.

Her mum bent down slightly behind Ailsa. 'Go on, my love,' she whispered into her ear. She gave Ailsa the lightest of pushes towards Camilla. 'We'll be in the car. Take your time.'

'Aye, then,' Ailsa muttered. She walked up to Camilla as everyone else climbed into the car.

Neither of them knew what to do. It felt strained. Ailsa felt awkward. She didn't know what she could possibly say to Camilla to make everything all right. Then Moxie barged her out the way, bounding forwards. He leaped up at Camilla, putting his forepaws on her shoulders and smothering her face with one wet, long lick.

'Argh!' Camilla squealed.

Then Ailsa was laughing. Camilla began to laugh, too. She wrapped her arms around Moxie, gave him a big squeeze and then ruffled her hands through his fur. The big Shepherd nuzzled in, burying his face into the crook of her neck, panting and licking as he wagged his tail in excitement.

'Come on, boy,' Ailsa said at last.

Moxie dropped, still wagging, and left the two girls looking at one another.

'Hi,' Ailsa said.

'Hi,' Camilla said. Her lower lip quivered. Great, fat tears gathered on her eyelashes. She sniffed and sobbed, then she took a step towards Ailsa.

Ailsa opened her arms. Camilla fell forward, into Ailsa's embrace. She sobbed and sobbed. She buried her face deep in Ailsa's hair. Her legs were weak, and Ailsa had to half hold her up. She gathered Camilla in, holding her close as she wept.

They stood there, like that, for a long, long time.

'A-hem,' Uncle Nod said pointedly after a while. He was leaning out of the car window, looking at them. 'There's plenty of food.'

'Aye,' Mum piped up from the back, looking at Camilla. 'You'd be more than welcome to come along.'

'R-really?' Camilla asked, gazing into Ailsa's eyes.

'Don't be silly,' Ailsa said. 'Of course. It'd be lovely. And you can meet my mum. Properly, you know?'

Twenty-six

They set up for their picnic on a high, hilly clifftop a couple of miles away. It was a bit of a sludgy drive to get up to the top. The rain had churned the hillside to mud over the last few days. But when they arrived, the whole island opened up to them. They could see it all. The sea stretched out seemingly for ever below them, dancing with the sunlight, deep blue and tranquil.

'Crikey,' Uncle Nod said.

Ailsa looked at the back of the car, at the wheels. Thick mud clung to everything.

'I half thought we were going to have to get out and push!'

The hilltop itself was dry, though. Ailsa, Camilla and Moxie ran up ahead and found a perfect spot near a cliff edge. There were a couple of trees casting a nice shade, and Ailsa nodded, decided.

'For Mum, for her skin, you know,' Ailsa explained to Camilla. 'She's been inside too much. She can't be out in full sunlight.'

'Are you two going to help out, or just charge about all day?' Aunt Bertha called over to them.

Looking around, Ailsa saw her aunt, her mum and Uncle Nod all struggling along with the picnic things.

'Oh, right, aye,' she said.

She and Camilla jogged back over, grabbed a thick blanket and a couple of cushions, and laid it all out half under the trees' shade.

Uncle Nod dished lunch out to them. He had a box of sandwiches for them to begin with, and they all launched themselves eagerly into them.

'It's all delicious,' Camilla said, tucking into her third.

'He always likes to show off to company,' Ailsa said through a mouthful of shrimp mayonnaise. 'Cooking, like, you know?'

Aunt Bertha laughed out loud, a great, snorting snigger.

257

Ailsa's mum chuckled and Camilla smiled. Moxie simply howled and wagged.

'Aye, well,' Uncle Nod grumbled. He looked at Ailsa's mum. 'I think she's turning into a teenager already.'

They finished the sandwiches, then started in on the rest, some cakes and crisps, some fruit lying forgotten to one side. Uncle Nod kept on producing food until they were groaning, until their bellies grew full and heavy, and their heads grew thick and sleepy.

The warm sun and the smell of the sea seemed to quiver with life around them all. It got into Ailsa's lungs and into her head. It got behind her eyes until they couldn't help but close. Unable to hold it at bay any longer, Ailsa fell asleep as the afternoon wore on. So did Camilla. Sleepless nights and the stress of the last few days caught up with them both.

She woke up briefly, partly, a couple of times.

The first time, she was lying beside Moxie on the picnic blanket. Her mum and Uncle Nod were quietly chatting a little way off. They had serious looks on their faces, though they were wistful as they stared out across the sea. Aunt Bertha was humming quietly to herself as she picked at a slice of cake. Camilla was snoring loudly, lounging in the warm grass a little way off.

The second time, she was curled up in her mum's arms. Camilla was awake, gazing out to sea, as Aunt Bertha and Uncle Nod spoke to her.

'It'll be all right in the end,' Uncle Nod was telling Camilla.

Camilla nodded and half mumbled in reply.

'These things are never that bad, no matter how they look,' he carried on. 'They'll be able to rebuild, put things back together.'

'They'll have insurance, too, your mum and dad,' Aunt Bertha added. 'So it'll all be paid for. You can either fix the house up or your mum can buy somewhere new. Your mum and dad can, that is.'

'Aye, a fresh start with money in the bank,' Uncle Nod said. 'You can't argue with that.'

'I think I would like that,' Camilla said in quite a small voice. 'A fresh start,' she whispered.

Ailsa was only half listening, however. It all felt so wonderful. She wanted it to go on for ever. She curled tighter into her mum's arms. She nuzzled in, pushing deeply against her mum's chest, into the softness of her hair.

'Oh, love,' her mum whispered. She squeezed Ailsa a little more tightly and stroked her hair with one hand.

Later, Ailsa spent a long time sitting on the cliffs, gazing out at the sea as the sun began to dip down to the horizon. The ferries shepherding folk to the mainland and back chugged along, their wakes broad and full of slow fury. She imagined she heard Hefring's song, though really it was just the sound of the cool breeze and the waves crashing lazily below.

It's the same thing, though, she thought. *Hefring's song is the song of the sea. The song of the sea is Hefring's song.*

So she sat looking over the waves, listening, feeling close to Hefring.

'You're thinking about her?' Camilla asked, coming to sit next to her.

Everyone else was on the picnic blanket a way off, lounging in the last of the day's sunshine, picking intermittently at whatever food was left over. Her mum was lying propped up on one elbow in the trees' shade.

'Aye,' Ailsa said. 'Just listening out, you know?'

'Yes,' Camilla said. Her eyes were still a little swollen with the tears she had shed over the last couple of days. Her cheeks were pale. But she looked peaceful as she sat down next to Ailsa and listened to the waves.

'You OK?' Ailsa asked.

Camilla shrugged.

'I thought, you know, you'd be angry with Hefring.'

'What for?' Camilla asked.

'Well, isn't it obvious?' Ailsa replied, speaking gently. 'We get her sea-skin back to her, then that same night your house falls in and your dad's arrested. It's a bit of a coincidence, isn't it?'

'I know what you're saying,' Camilla said, still gazing out, her eyes on the horizon. 'And yes, I think you're right. It's no coincidence. But Daddy had it coming. He has done for a while. For ever, maybe, him and the rest of my family.

'I love them all,' she carried on with a sigh. 'I'll always love them. And I'll even miss him, I think, if he goes to prison or anything like that. But I know the kind of family we are. Daddy always called himself a businessman, but that's only ever been a small part of it. Gangsters, all of us, the Galachs. That's what everyone says, and they are right. And he's the worst of the lot.'

'Do you still want to work for their firm when you leave school?' Ailsa asked.

Camilla shook her head. 'No,' she said. 'I don't think there will be a firm, to be honest. But apart from that, no. I don't want any part in any of that. I want a proper job, a job doing something good. I don't want to be a gangster.'

'You'll have to start doing your schoolwork,' Ailsa said, smiling at Camilla. 'At that posh school of yours. You know, if you want to get a proper job.'

Camilla laughed ruefully. 'Yes, well, we'll see about that, won't we.' Camilla looked over at Ailsa's mum, then. 'She looks good,' she said. 'Tired, you know, but good.'

'Aye,' Ailsa said. She looked at Camilla and she looked at her mum. They were both pale, both made ragged and thin. But they were both strong, she thought.

Her mum's eyes were shining, dancing in the sunlight as she laughed at one of Uncle Nod's jokes. Aunt Bertha rolled her own eyes, and both she and Ailsa's mum collapsed about, laughing even harder.

She remembered what Uncle Nod had said just a little while ago.

. . . your ma's always been one of the strongest people I've ever known. Real iron in her blood, you know?

Aye, Ailsa thought. Her mum struggled with life, but that didn't mean too much in the end. It didn't really change who she was. She always came round from it, though rarely as quickly or as immediately as she had this time.

But Hefring is free, the song is free, she thought. *Mum heard it. It woke her own song up, gave her the strength she needed, showed her the world's beauty.*

And her eyes shone with it. They were alive. On this wonderful, glorious day, they were alive.

Acknowledgements

First things first, we need to talk about Bella Pearson. She *is* Guppy – its founder, its brains, its heart and soul. Thank you so much for plucking me out of thin air and putting my story on these pages. Guppy is an astonishing company and a wonderful collaborator. I can think of no one with whom I would rather swim against the tide.

Tamsin Rosewell comes next. Thank you for putting up with my garbled cues. Thank you for reading my story and interpreting it so beautifully on these covers. I might have invented Hefring, but you brought her to life.

Thank you, thank you.

I also want to mention Jenny Savill of Andrew Nurnberg Associates, my agent. You saw the potential for more than a one-hit-wonder. Here's to proving you right in the coming years (fingers crossed.) Thank you for your leap of faith.

My professional life is only a small part of things. What makes me a writer is more than an industry family. It takes a real family to bring out the magic.

This book is dedicated to my parents, Liz and David, who taught me to love books before I could even talk, who taught me to read before I even got to school. My brother, Adam, has been one of my greatest friends and a wonderful source of support and comfort over the years. My nans, too, Betty and Norma, deserve a great deal of thanks and as much love as I can express. You have always made my life warmer and kinder.

Thanks, too, to Rebecca and George for being children with me. And thanks are also due to Tattie for keeping me young, though she might not know it!

When I got married, I took on a few extra family members. Thank you to Gay and Paul for your untiring support.

Writing takes growth and expansion. It requires you to challenge yourself. With this in mind, I would like to express my admiration for the Open University. They have given me a great many years of joy, stimulation, and development, from ignorant undergrad to ignorant master's graduate.

But I have left the best till last. Above all, thank you Lauren, for being everything. We laugh, and we laugh, and we laugh.

Thank you all.

NAME OF
THE DOG

Also by Élmer Mendoza in English translation

Silver Bullets (2015)

The Acid Test (2016)